RESURRECTING FLEDGLING

The Sequel

JACK WEITZEL,
with
Michael Weitzel RT,
Lisa Weitzel RN CRM
and
Dr. Ken Weitzel

ISBN 978-1-68517-436-1 (paperback)
ISBN 978-1-68517-437-8 (digital)

Christian Faith Publishing, Inc.
832 Park Avenue
Meadville, PA 16335
www.christianfaithpublishing.com

Printed in the United States of America

INTRODUCTION

At the start of the third millennium anno Domini and the twenty-first century, another rural hospital in America closes along with its town. Looking toward the future, the San Petra Corporation, a group of dedicated ecumenical Christians, chooses the town of Fledgling, USA, to be ground zero for the development of medical care for the future of America. A pine tree forest is harvested along with 180 acres of farmland from a citizen's last will and testament. In their place by the second decade, a medical community arises which will change the face of medicine for the future in America, starting with the town of Fledgling, USA. A billion-dollar project with private funds and the story of Lazarus brought to life. An unrivaled medical complex arises out of the dust. Across the nation, rural towns are revived, if not resurrected.

Alex Martin's life had experienced the miracle of knowing Jesus. The apostle Paul's life arose out of the dust as well from the meeting with Jesus on the dusty road to Damascus. He was among those haters of Jesus, those who brought about His death on the terrible cross of Calvary. But Paul and the other disciples—a group made up of fisherman, a tax collector, and others that nobody would ever think were capable—turned the world upside down after the death of their leader.

"Therefore if any man be in Christ, he is a new creature: old things are passed away; behold, all things are become new" (2 Corinthians 5:17). Case in point, Alex Martin.

Paul went on to be the writer of nearly one third of the New Testament. Alex Martin, PhD, met Jesus on his near-death bed as he struggled in need of both a heart transplant and a soul transplant. A charismatic, born-again Catholic priest (unbeknown to be his thirty-two-year-old son, born out of wedlock) led Alex to saving faith in Jesus Christ just before losing his life in a tragic accident but not before giving his father his heart.

Paul had been the enemy of Jesus, dragging believers to prison. The apostle's reputation frightened those in his world…too big a miracle, too enormous the change. Likewise, Alex's postconversion life was met with skepticism. Family and friends couldn't understand nor accept this changed life, and so family and friends just considered Alex just another "wackjob" Jesus freak and basically distanced themselves. It was two-three years before postconversion Paul was accepted by the apostles and those following the apostles. As Paul in his world was a strong witness for the Lord, personally having met him, so Alex's new life was a game changer.

Alex was still a young man of fifty-two post-heart transplant. He had become the ultimate good father donating one of his kidneys to his dying son James, a victim of kidney failure. Alex and Hannah took over as parents to these two boys, James and John, who had been indoctrinated into the Jehovah's Witness faith. It was the prayers and study of what they were dealing with, a *cult* by mainstream Christianity, that ultimately led the two boys to faith in Jesus.

Alex had been the crème of the crop of biology professors in academia; his textbook, for years, was studied by high schoolers and especially college kids. His most popular biology textbook was sans any mention of anything of God, except belief in the Darwinian theory of evolution and as far as creation, the big bang, or aliens from another planet leaving off life before they left.

Alex clearly wanted to show his love for the Lord through a textbook, rewriting the truth of the creation story as he had now come to believe it. Alex believed that he had a divine mission to develop a godly biology textbook, unashamed to discuss topics such as biblical creation alongside Darwinism and other theories to be studied in high school before entering liberal colleges. His own two sons, victims of indoctrination in the JW faith, through their parents' prayers, were able to change their worldview. It wasn't smooth sailing or a slam dunk, but in New Fledgling, the school board allowed the new biology text in homeschoolers and in Madison High School. Writing a God-honoring biology textbook would eventually be found in virtual biology classes. The process took three years.

Interesting tangent to the truth, the way, and the life, Alex found himself in the same Sunday school class taught by Paula Hunter. Surrounded by Christian friends, Paula asked for prayer, intercessory prayer in the life of her twin sister Laura who was raised in a non-Christian home. She spent several weeks discussing the sixth chapter of the letter to the church in Ephesus, including the armor of God.

> Finally, my brethren, be strong in the Lord, and in the power of his might. Put on the whole armour of God, that ye may be able to stand against the wiles of the devil. For we wrestle not against flesh and blood, but against principalities, against powers, against the rulers of the darkness of this world, against spiritual wickedness in high places. Wherefore take unto you the whole armour of God, that ye may be able to withstand in the evil day, and having done all, to stand. Stand therefore, having your loins girt about with truth, and having on the breastplate of righteousness; and your feet shod with the preparation of the gospel of peace. Above all, taking the shield of faith, wherewith ye shall be able to quench all the fiery darts of the wicked. And take the helmet of salvation, and the sword of the Spirit, which is the word of God: Praying always with all prayer and supplication in the Spirit and watching thereunto with all perseverance and supplication for all saints. (Ephesians 6:10–18 KJV)

Is the Bible just a book of fantasy? In a 2015 survey, the National Association of Evangelicals found that 63 percent of Christians accepted Jesus Christ between the ages of four and fourteen. This stage of life is a window of opportunity for the church where the harvest is plentiful (Matthew 9:37).

Missiologists often speak of the need for the church to reach the ten to forty window. The church also needs to be mindful of the four to fourteen window.

The four to fourteen window is not only the time when a child is most likely to embrace the gospel, but also when they will form an emotional impression of church. Not all children will receive the gospel during their four to fourteen window, and some may even leave the church during their young adult years. But one of the most important determinants of a returning churchgoer will be the quality of the deposit the church made during the child's formative years. If there was no church involvement or an unhealthy experience in those early years, they may never come to a saving grace. For instance, you might hear, "My parents made me go to church and Sunday school until I left for college, and I hated it!"

In the Parable of the Prodigal Son (Luke 15:11–24), the wayward son eventually becomes desperate and comes to his senses. At this moment, he remembers the kindness of his father and determines to return home. The church must prepare the hearts of the children for the time when they come to their senses: a person who leaves home and behaves recklessly but later makes a repentant return to faith in Christ. Remember how the father looked earnestly for the wayward son. It wasn't just by coincidence that the father just happened to be out on that day watching for his son. No, God is looking all the time for the child to return to his Christian heritage, and when that happens, there is great rejoicing in heaven. For he was lost and was now found, was blind and now could see the truth. It often takes total surrender for a person to trust in the Lord as their Savior and their Lord.

In Luke 15:11–24, the Parable of the Prodigal Son, Jesus taught mainly in parables.

> And he said, a certain man had two sons: And the younger of them said to his father, Father, give me the portion of goods that falleth

> to me. And he divided unto them his living. And not many days after the younger son gathered all together, and took his journey into a far country, and there wasted his substance with riotous living. And when he had spent all, there arose a mighty famine in that land; and he began to be in want. And he went and joined himself to a citizen of that country; and he sent him into his fields to feed swine. And he would fain have filled his belly with the husks that the swine did eat and no man gave unto him. And when he came to himself, he said, how many hired servants of my fathers have bread enough and to spare, and I perish with hunger! I will arise and go to my father, and will say unto him, Father, I have sinned against heaven, and before thee, and am no more worthy to be called thy son: make me as one of thy hired servants. And he arose and came to his father. But when he was yet a great way off, his father saw him, and had compassion, and ran, and fell on his neck, and kissed him. And the son said unto him, Father, I have sinned against heaven, and in thy sight, and am no more worthy to be called thy son. But the father said to his servants, bring forth the best robe, and put it on him; and put a ring on his hand, and shoes on his feet: And bring hither the fatted calf, and kill it; and let us eat, and be merry: For this my son was dead, and is alive again; he was lost, and is found. And they began to be merry.

That's heavens angels rejoicing and celebrating whenever someone becomes saved and gives their heart to the Lord Jesus. In Luke 15:7, Jesus continued, "I say unto you, that likewise joy shall be in heaven over one sinner that repenteth." He was referring to the shepherd with one hundred sheep, and at the end of the day, the count is only ninety-nine. He leaves to find the lost sheep and returns rejoicing.

Sometimes Paula would phone Laura, and someone would answer, and the background noise suggested a party going on. That had happened more than once. Laura seemed to be a social person. Paula was always left with the wonder of who were in the inner circle of her sister, but she was never invited to any of Laura's gatherings. That's a bit strange!

Was Laura a lost soul? Yes! Paula would never give up praying for her lost sister. Only time will tell.

Some forty miles away to the north of New Fledgling, the Veterans Hospital, which had opened its doors in 1972, has begun to fade away with the last of the Vietnam veterans, the baby boomers passing away or are soon to retire. It's a different facility seventy years later and has downsized considerably. The VH now faces further hurdles that could prove fatal to its existence.

Prologue

The Hunters, Jeffrey and Audrey, were driving homeward after spending three wonderful spring days at Disney World in Orlando. Twelve-year-old son Bobbie and the ten-year-old identical twin girls were in the back seat asleep. Nearing sundown, they were coming to an intersection with a green light. Their vehicle was struck broadside at sixty miles an hour by a tow truck in a hurry, instantly taking the lives of Mom and Dad and Bobbie. Bobbie flew from the back seat through the front windshield, breaking his neck. Paula was thrown against the left rear door, sustaining left lower rib fractures which ruptured her spleen and broke her left humerus. Laura sustained right chest wall trauma with multiple right lower rib fractures, a lacerated liver, and pelvic fractures. Both girls had significant facial lacerations. Neither girl would remember the accident itself.

EMS were on the scene quickly; jaws of life were needed to get everyone out of the vehicle. They were transported to a nearby level 1 trauma center with excellent pediatric trauma care as well. Both girls required rapid resuscitative measures and extensive surgery with subsequent long-term intensive care in the pediatric intensive care unit.

(A funeral was held at their Baptist church outside of New Fledgling for their parents and brother. Oh, such a somber event in a steady drizzle.)

The twins were hospitalized for over two weeks. Jeff's mother and his older sister practically lived at this hospital three hundred miles from their homes near Fledgling. During that time, Jeff's mother had decided that ideally the twins should stay together. The godly grandmother wanted to raise them under her roof. So upon discharge, they went home with Grandma Irene. Aunt Polly's home was thirty miles away from New Fledgling. There was a problem with

Laura needing intense rehabilitation for her pelvic fractures. Aunt Polly was closer to the rehab center, so they thought it best for Laura to stay with her father's older sister Polly. The center was just thirty minutes from Polly's home. Polly had a fiancée who happened to be an attorney and was able to sue the company that owned the truck and its driver. Along with the children's parents' life insurance policies, they were financially in a good way. Carl, Polly's fiancée, assisted in setting up a trust for the girls for their future.

Paula was raised in a Christian home and attended all private Christian schools through college where she studied and received a bachelor's degree in nursing. She had attended the local Baptist church with Grandma all through her childhood with Irene leading Paula to a saving relationship with Jesus Christ in the sixth grade. Paula had strong faith and would depend upon that relationship to guide her through the future. After college, Paula enlisted in the navy and had an illustrious twenty-year career with one long tour of duty aboard the *USS Mercy*, a year in Afghanistan, and back in the States at Bethesda Naval Hospital. She advanced through the ranks to captain at the time of her retirement. She continued the military theme at the Veterans Hospital, an hour's drive from New Fledgling. She began as a floor nurse and a situation arose that began her career as director of a busy Central Supply adjacent to a twenty-operating room surgical suite.

Laura, on the other hand, was raised by Polly to know that there was a God but anything beyond that were existential questions we all must deal with. She would allow Laura to answer those questions for herself as time goes by. She attended the neighborhood schools and a liberal arts university away from home, studying nursing with a minor in abnormal psychology. She obtained a master's degree in clinical psychology as well as becoming a registered nurse. After her education, she applied to the teaching hospital in Fledgling (soon to be called New Fledgling). The hospital had just opened its first three floors, and the opportunities at the new medical complex were extremely attractive to a new nurse. She also quickly moved through the system with a position in the emergency room and worked hard which paid off as she became SICU charge nurse and advanced to director of nursing services.

Paula retired from the navy, and the twins, for a short time, lived together in New Fledgling at Laura's home in the Shady Acres Development near the New Fledgling medical complex. After a few months, Paula moved to a place of her own, closer to the VH. What made them decide to live apart? Just simply more convenient? Well, that certainly was a part of the decision, but lifestyles and worldviews were the overwhelming reason, and it went as far back as the twins not living together during their childhood, Paula having been raised by the grandmother while Laura lived with the free-spirited Aunt Polly and her fiancé. A great deal to do with nurture and less due to do with nature. Although not living together, they would visit each other and share what they were up to. It was the last year of high school when their different personalities made it clear who the twins were.

As it turns out, Paula was the shy, dedicated-to-the-church, born-again believer who was content to study hard and succeed, while Laura was more sociable, academics was of less importance for her, and she was popular in high school with an adventurous soul (a lost soul).

Those few months in New Fledgling when they lived together were awkward. Laura was often going to parties, leaving Paula comfortably alone but puzzled when Laura stayed out late; usually Paula would be in bed by nine to ten o'clock with Laura coming in at all hours. She often waited up when it appeared that Laura had been drinking at some party and getting behind the wheel. The proverbial good girl, bad girl. Paula was at church or some related church activity every Wednesday from 6:00 to 9:00 p.m. Midweek worship was important to Paula.

One Wednesday, Paula had her usual supper at the church but had developed a bad headache and had gone home early. The driveway was overflowing with vehicles unfamiliar to her. Perhaps one of the neighbors was having a meeting. Nearing the front door of the home, loud music could be heard. The front door locked, Paula opened it with her card key and found nearly a dozen women she had never met before, total strangers. A few of the girls were dancing together, some were drinking alcohol and smoking (and not just cigarettes) something very unusual for Laura to be involved with. After saying hello and claiming a bad headache, she went straight to her bedroom. The music died down, and Paula had a restless sleep. In the morning, she discussed what she had seen and let Laura know that she in no way could support Laura's lifestyle and live this way. It was Laura's home. Paula told her that she would be looking for a place to live nearer to the Veterans Hospital. Within a week, Paula bought a home close to the VH.

As they advanced during the subsequent years, each had significant responsibilities and were well respected by their personnel. Paula was still busy with her Sunday church attendance as well as teaching an adult coed class. Her schedule was set. She was off every Wednesday afternoon and evening and every Sunday for services. Laura skipped hump day as well as Sunday to rest.

The identicality of twins can be transient and altered by the vicissitudes of life, the nature versus nurture question. Despite all of that, if you saw them together, you would know they still were identical twins. Laura had a slight limp from muscle damage from her pelvic fractures when she was ten years old. From a distance, you could not tell them apart.

1

If I could hazard a guess at some point in time, you have come across the phrase "Back in the day." That phrase is an American idiom used to refer to an earlier time fondly remembered. The VH of 2042 was not the Veterans Hospital (VH) of the 1970s: middle-aged and older men lounging around in their government issued pajamas; everyone smoking (in a hospital?) and playing cards and just wandering aimlessly; just waiting, going to the commissary for smokes, waiting for it to be their turn for the overdue haircut. It got so busy the university had to start a medical school across the street. Waiting was usually greater than two to three weeks of this aimlessness for any elective procedure like a hernia repair and some longer. For the navy guys, it was just like being aboard ship off the coast. Some emergency cases unfortunately had been kept waiting too long. Activated in 1972, the VH is a tertiary care facility classified as a Clinical Referral Level 1 (not trauma) Facility. VH is a teaching hospital, providing a full range of patient care services, with state-of-the-art technology as well as education and research.

Waiting, for instance in the mid-1970s, the sad case of the fifty-five-year-old veteran found to have a large abdominal aortic aneurysm. The size kept murmured to be enlarging, as they twiddled or fiddled. (The noninvasive surgical repair of operative diseases began just shy of the year 1983. This was roughly 1978.) There were two gown vascular surgeon (before vascular surgery was recognized with board certification) attendings who put this patient off for nearly a month. Getting the resident, who thought that he was fully prepared for this, only for the attendings to back out because of "scheduling conflicts." They waited until this asymptomatic retired navy cook began having to complain of some back pain. It quickly became more severe, agonizing pain and shock. A collective *oh no*! They got him to the operating room where he did not have much of a blood pressure. As soon as they made the incision, it was too late. All the surgeons' shoes were full of blood. No family. Somehow this case never made it to any morbidity/mortality Saturday morning conference. The blame belonged somewhere, but no one would accept it. (Just a sample case.) AAA treatment since the 2020s has been noninvasively done with ever decreasing morbidity and mortality.

Add to the hubbub the short white-coated medical students, the long white-coated residents, and all the dependents and nursing services and the seven-story, seven hundred-bed VH was indeed remembered fondly. Surgical admissions were 14,000 per year with 2,000 surgical procedures per year in 1981: 50 full-time physicians, 68 attending physicians, and 32 consultants (from the Bulletin College of Medicine 1981–1982). Much later, the medical school would subsequently make its own move downtown and the VH not so busy as the center for teaching but still very viable, hanging on.

With the last of the Vietnam veterans nearly gone, the VH seemed destined to pass along with them. Veterans checked in to the hospital, had their procedures done on schedule, and were discharged routinely within a matter of days, even as routine as the monthly grand rounds lectures to bore you to tears if you could stay awake. The fact that the facility was forty or so miles north did not deter anyone for there were comfortable living facilities for those on call or wanting to basically camp out there with their sick patients. It was still alive! This turnaround was at the reins of Donald J. Trump, the forty-fifth president of the United States of America. For many reasons, there is a long list of his campaign promises he made right in 2016–2020. He needed the American election process to survive without frank fraud. The election stolen from seventy million plus Americans who voted legally for him in 2020.

The monthly Monday 7:00 a.m. VH Surgical Grand Rounds topic had been scratched off the schedules on the doors to the lecture hall and in their place someone with a surgeon's dry sense of humor and a red magic marker sharpie had written "Surgical Grand Rounds cancelled; next month's topic will be 'Surgery of the Thyroid by Dr. Graves (of Grave's Disease)'" Thyroidectomy, or the complete or partial removal of the thyroid gland, is *the least common* form of treatment of Graves' disease. It is usually reserved for people with very enlarged thyroids, also known as a goiter or pregnant women who haven't reacted well to antithyroid medicines. People with nothing to do had nothing better to do than to try and figure out what to do for that hour's reprieve. The men and women in green scrubs usually there in some number were absent, and there was a buzz about the room from the remaining *fleas* and attendings and students.

Chief Surgical Resident Rob Rogers stepped to the podium announcing to those in attendance and in the dark what the situation was. This is what he explained:

The prior Monday, the (partial) operating room schedule looked like this:

> Room 2, 38 YO male laparoscopic cholecystectomy (LC) Dr. A
> Room 4, 47 YO male laparoscopic asst. sigmoid colectomy (SC) Dr. B
> Room 6, 53 YO female laparoscopic hysterectomy (LH) Dr. C
> Room 8, 56 YO female laparoscopic total hysterectomy (LTAH) Dr. D
> Room 10, 40 YO male open RT adrenalectomy (OA) Dr. E

All surgical cases were done under general anesthesia in different rooms by different surgeons. Patients were both male and female in different ages. There were no apparent intraoperative complications. All patients' immediate postoperative courses were uneventful. They were discharged from hospital between twenty-four to seventy-two hours. Operative reports were available in the patients' charts and were reviewed and were unremarkable.

Between day 5 and day 6 of postop, all five of these patients trickling in were admitted through the VH emergency room with chief complaint of headache, fever, chills, severe abdominal pain, and borderline, low blood pressures. Upon admission to the SICU, all patients were alert and cooperative, looking acutely ill, with the above complaints. Their admission overflowed to the MICU on the same second floor. The operative surgeons were notified and promptly gave orders to the ward secretary. All surgeons (or their nurse practitioners or physician's assistants) arrived at the VH in a timely fashion. The picture was one of pandemonium. This event was near catastrophic in the history of this Veterans Hospital! These patients were all in dire straits, possibly septic. All presented about the same, low blood pressure with tachycardia and worsening abdominal pain, low urinary output, confusion. Any time wasted thinking that they could handle all these desperately ill patients would lead to a grave (no pun intended) situation. These patients needed to be transferred to the teaching hospital's Trauma Institute. Transportation was being rapidly mobilized.

The hospital's resources were quickly overwhelmed. It was immediately apparent that this hospital could not handle this quantity and quality of extremely ill patients who were getting sicker by the hour, and they all needed intensive care. Maybe back in 1981 it could be handled but not now with a skeleton crew compared to six decades ago. They all needed a greater degree of assistance than the VH could provide. One or two sick patients was one thing, but five at the same time, they believed, would only lead to tragedy. This crisis was way over their collective heads. This, at one time, had been an all-too-busy VH, a main teaching hospital with all resources. They were no longer the teaching hospital they once were, but they still had their small contingent of residents and medical students. Most of the surgery done at the VH were a dozen or so cases per week, usually early in the week. This past Monday had been an exception with the two retired nurses adding to the mix. They had to import gynecologists from the town to help in training the VH doctors. Downsizing included the surgical suite which only used ten of its operating rooms.

Suzanne Grayson, MD, had agreed to help the VH gynecologists with the necessary training. She had been one of the last gynecologists to deliver babies. She and her partner, Dr. Veronica Lacy, were agreeable to assisting. No longer could they be referred to as OB-GYN doctors. There were two VH gynecologists on staff who had not been fully trained in laparoscopic procedures, needing to complete their training (ten supervised cases on videotape assisted by one fully trained). That was the job of Doctors Grayson and Lacy from the teaching hospital. What has happened to obstetrics? Too many "bad babies" and multimillion-dollar lawsuits over too many years. Midwifery and nurse practitioners were filling the void starting in the early decades of the new century. There are programs with yearly dues accumulating over time which becomes a buffer or resource for those desiring to stick with the OB practice, who really enjoyed delivering babies.

In one state, all physicians with few exceptions are required to pay the Birth-Related Neurological Injury Compensation Association (NICA) fee. NICA ensures that birth-injured children and adults receive the care they need while reducing the financial burden on medical providers and families. The NICA plan is funded by annual assessments to participating physicians and hospitals. Obstetric physicians and midwives are eligible to participate in the NICA plan by paying the required $5,000 fee each calendar year to help resolve catastrophic claims for birth-related injuries without lengthy and costly malpractice litigation. This was augmented by annual assessments paid statewide by *all* physicians and hospitals with few exceptions.

That Monday was reminiscent of the 1977 thriller by Robin Cook, *Coma*, made into a blockbuster movie by the same title. The Jefferson Institute is a black-market organ-harvesting ring, and carbon monoxide is used at Boston Memorial in OR 8 to provide more patients with more organs to sell. The culprit being the feed-in of an OR gas line causing coma. The patients in that same operating room afflicted were sent to an out-of-town hospice of sorts (the Jefferson Institute), a sterile holding place for comatose patients to be kept alive as a source for organ harvesting early on in transplant history. This was an international source for livers, hearts, and kidneys for the most part. Soft music in the background until you got closer to the suspended people with the soft mechanical sound of ventilators overshadowing the music. Hundreds of thousands of dollars passed through that *hospice*.

Whatever happened in 2042 has implicated the entire surgical suite and not just one room but the beginnings of a catastrophe.

(The awaited-for case had arrived. Sunday, dark-thirty... They knew about the location of all the surveillance cameras. There were no cameras in the specimen room. There was a camera's blind spot behind one of the giant autoclaves in Central Supply. There were cameras along all the hallways in every operating room and in 80 percent of Central Supply, especially right next to the entrance. Hopefully, they can disarm the camera's system if the "toggle switch" could be found. [It had recently undergone rewiring because the system had shorted out.] The camera's field of vision did not include the entrance to the surgical suite. It had been moved from its original position. A quick search under the counter and it was about a foot from the original spot at the receiving entrance where it could be easily turned on and off by the crew before leaving for the evening. The camera's system disabled, all that was needed was less than thirty minutes. The "cup" with the purulent drainage from the sergeant's abscess was still there. Sixty CCS of the sergeant's drainage was pulled up into a syringe and slipped into the side-coat pocket of the white lab coat, taking less than a minute. It was as quiet as a church mouse. Now to Central Supply. The long silver table with the instrument packs was where it always is, outside room 1. It was rolled to CS. The packs found according to the surgical schedule, the wrapping unfolded, and instruments exposed. An aerosolized mixture of unsterile saline and the sergeant's abscess material was sprayed on the instruments of the five opened packs. Only half of the mixture was used. A careful rewrap of the packs was done; the sterilization tapes were reapplied. The table rolled back into its position along the wall by OR 1. On the way out, the toggle switch was switched to the on position. The process had taken less than thirty minutes. Everything looked as though no one had been there. Dark-thirty Sunday night, one week ago.)

The VH system having downsized, a point was reached that significantly ill ICU patients quickly overwhelmed the system. In the current situation, it was felt reasonable to transfer these patients to facilities more capable of caring for them, giving them the best chance and hope for recovery. It was known for a fact that the teaching hospital of New Fledgling provided the best chance of recovery for this type of scenario. The chief of staff of the VH, Dr. Brice Adams, Capt., USN, did not hesitate and quickly made the call deciding for transfer to New Fledgling (NF). Dr. Adams is a fifty-eight-year-old boarded intensivist/psychiatrist anticipating new orders over the next three to six months hopefully as commander of one of the US Navy's hospital ships. He has been COS at the VH for ten years ready for a change of venue. Brice Adams has been married to Celeste for fifteen years, and they have no children. Celeste is a pediatric surgeon at the teaching hospital in New Fledgling. They each have heavy-duty jobs and have become as ships passing in the night.

Captain Adams has had an interesting social life for the past two years. He plays golf on Wednesday afternoons two or three times a month with a woman named Sondra. She is an attractive, shapely, brown-haired, heavily made-up forty-eight-year-old psychologist he had met at a conference three years earlier. After playing golf, they have diner, and after which, they both go to their separate ways after a brief hug, purely a platonic relationship. On Wednesdays, he drives a leased white Chevrolet van; otherwise, he drives his jaguar. He does feel an element of guilt and anxiety about this… Sondra is a friend to talk with. Brice rarely sees his wife, Celeste. These past several years have been a challenge for the couple to keep their marriage alive. They might just as well be *separated*. They have lost much of the love of the earlier years in their relationship…drifting apart as the years go by. Sad to see.

Medevac helicopters were already in flight. The arrangements had been made rather quickly without any significant workup having been done at the VH. They were afraid to waste valuable time. They did, however, have CBCs drawn showing markedly elevated white blood cell counts consistent with inflammation and high enough to corroborate clinical presentations. One exception was the laparoscopically assisted colon resection. It was obvious this patient probably needed reoperation for a supposed anastomotic leak, and he was taken straight to the VH radiology department where a gentle gastrografin enema revealed an intact anastomosis. He was found to have a pelvic abscess which was drained, and patient sent to the SICU for further evaluation and treatment.

After transfer of the four patients to New Fledgling, the entire weekend had been spent going over everything that could conceivably have caused this. All the rooms were cultured especially the anesthesia equipment and ventilators. All the staff personnel and surgeons enjoyed a very hectic weekend with interviews of all by the chief of nursing and infectious disease personnel. It was a far cry from the Spanish inquisition. There had been other cases being done in those rooms during the rest of that week without incident—just those patients from the Monday schedule were involved. Initial thought of closing the operating suite was negated for how benign the courses were of patients operated upon the remainder of that week. That may have been a mistake!

2

The concept of the medical campus of New Fledgling (NF) had spread across the country. Graduating students from the Medical College of San Petra as per contract had been dispersed to various rural areas of the States, and the results were outstanding with spinoff strategies such as had occurred in NF with infrastructure resurrection and medical campuses coming to life. Some of these *experiments* did not quite pan out, but for most situations, enhanced medical care nearly exploded in America. The medical college now a four-year curriculum had just begun its twentieth year, now with 128 students matriculating each year, and though not tuition-free, the tuition was one third that of similar medical colleges, still making it attractive (as well as its great history of excellence). Always being cognizant of rural health care insufficiency, the school was urging graduating students and senior residents to locate in communities of need, but there was no longer any contract as there had been two decades ago. Its purpose had been served. Nurse practitioners and physician assistants were taking up the void left by a declining number of doctors in America. The year 2019 marked the first year in which the percentage of osteopathic and foreign-trained doctors surpassed the percentage of US trained medical doctors matching into primary care positions.

Two medevac choppers carried the four "desperately ill" patients to the medical campus in New Fledgling. The cruising speed of ambulance choppers was 120 miles per hour, so the flight back from the VH, forty or so miles away, took literally minutes. A trauma alert had been given. Helicopters found purchase on the nearby dedicated runway. The patients were first delivered to the trauma side of the institute. The staff gladly received the four patients who were awake and alert none yet requiring ventilatory assistance while surgical residents, intensivists, and nurses either assisted with their workup or awaited the Trauma Institute's findings. Blood pressure-wise, they were not responding to crystalloids (IV fluids). Their eyes on, the staff was encouraged by these four new patients...they still had something left to fight with, all in their late forties to early fifties; they were still *young*. The blood pressures were not responding 90–80/60, HR 100-110. All with low grade temperatures.

Rapid assessments were carried out which included CT scans of the abdomen and pelvis. Scanners were a part of the anatomy of the entrance to the Trauma Institute, just like years ago in airports passing though checkpoints before boarding a plane. The scan itself was now dynamic, viewing the entire body and showing active bleeding or free air and orthopedic injuries as well. Each of the CT scans was consistent with some form of inflammatory changes or frank abscess. The incision sites for these minimally invasive procedures were all erythematous, crepitant, and very tender. The patients were stabilized rapidly for presumed sepsis. Central IV lines were placed, Foley catheters inserted, all incisions cultured, blood cultured, AP chest x-rays done, broad spectrum antibiotics begun, and patiently (no pun intended) each patient underwent localization and successful CT guided drainage of pelvic abscesses and one sub hepatic abscess from the gallbladder surgery.

All patients had borderline low blood pressures and low concentrated urine output. Their central pressures were low and urine output not responding to crystalloids (IV fluids). Low flow dopamine was begun. All drainage procedures revealed this same purulence. With cultures pending, drainage tubes were left in place. On Gram's stain, there were both gram negative rods and gram-positive cocci. Within forty-eight hours, cultures were positive for Escherichia coli and Bacteroides fragilis as well as MRSA (methicillin-resistant Staphylococcus aureus). Sensitivities known; antibiotics were adjusted accordingly. The fifth patient who remained at the VH was also stabilized, and the cultures of his pelvic abscess grew the same bacteria.

Then suddenly they all stabilized, responding with increased urine output BP 100/75. Observed closely, they also were breathing more easily, and blood gases were normalizing. After another hour of close observation, they were able to be transferred to the surgical intensive care unit. Families had arrived and were having a prayer meeting in the large second floor chapel. The patients would be kept on antibiotics for probably ten days. They were able to sip on liquids and shortly begun on clear liquid diets. It appeared that all four of these patients unbelievably would survive what could very well have been lethal outcomes.

They were able to be discharged after the course of antibiotics. It was truly a miraculous recovery, and all were thanking God for his mercy. The presumed brief episode of sepsis was interesting, very unusual responding so quickly to aggressive treatment. It baffled those taking care of those patients. Truly the prayers of the righteous availed much. The chapel had been quite active during the early hours of medical intervention. Folks coming and going. Even the skeptics of the healing power of prayer were asking questions about faith and "scratching their heads."

3

The parking lot of the VH has been overflowing with the medical staff frightful and anxious to solve this horrible situation. The worst thing that can happen is a repeat, and currently they haven't a clue as to solving this bizarre mystery. Lives were at stake. The patients cared for at the teaching hospital was a canon-shot (not a bullet) dodged with the recovery of all patients involved. They were lucky this time, or better yet, they were blessed! There was celebration in the chapel of the teaching hospital in New Fledgling.

All involved personnel at the VH, having taken part in the care of those four patients who had been transferred, were breathing collective sighs of relief with news of the patients' recovering. The patient with the colon resection, who remained at the VH, likewise recovered. They had plenty of time to go over all the known facts in these cases. They were baffled and really had a degree of fear that unless the cause for these septic patients could be found, it might just happen again. Quite frankly, this VH staff was not at the top of their game when it came to dealing with such ill patients. They were what they were and usually were able to provide adequate care for a relatively inactive teaching facility. But not for mass casualty handling! The cultures taken from the one patient not transferred were identical with the four patients taken to the teaching hospital in New Fledgling.

It seemed most prudent for personnel to investigate all recent cases done in the OR over the past days and weeks to check for any infected case(s) with the same bacterial spectrum. Paula Hunter, director of Central Supply, was asked to look at the books of the previous weeks and to check the autoclaves' graphics over that period.

She also decided that it might be helpful to look and follow up on pathologic cultures submitted from OR to laboratory/pathology departments. All path specimens coming from the OR to the lab/path department are placed in a small offset room which communicates through a flap window and all specimens interface at this point unless too large a specimen.

For instance, consider the case of Sylvester Jones, a thirty-seven-year-old AA male who, now three weeks ago, presented with an acute surgical abdomen secondary to perforated gangrenous appendicitis who had developed a fecal fistula (drainage of stool through an incision). He remains in the hospital and was otherwise doing well. His cultures have grown E. coli and Bacteroides frag but no MRSA. He is now afebrile tolerating a diet. On Tuesday of this week, Sgt. Pat Polcy was emergently operated on for a large perirectal abscess. He was drained Saturday in the VH OR and again Tuesday after clinic. (His original culture reports somehow disappeared as did the specimen. He died from septic shock. Much more about the sergeant later.)

Central Supply Departments are near or usually attached to the surgical suite, and in our case, it's twenty (now ten) operating rooms. An outside laundry service is responsible for cleaning all nondisposables such as drapes and towels, gowns and cloth materials used to wrap the surgical instrument packs prior to sterilization. Paper wrapping took over for the most part, and in 2042, nearly everything is disposable even some of the laparoscopic instruments. (And to tell the truth, some of the laparoscopists—those unable to master hand/eye coordination who had not been into computer gaming as a child.)

Depending on the institute, quite often Central Supply is also responsible for the cleaning of the surgical instruments postoperatively. There are cards posted (like recipes) telling what instruments are to go into which pack for what procedure. They set up the trays, wrap them and sterilize them in their four huge STERIS autoclaves. There were also autoclaves in the sub-sterile areas between the operating rooms and two smaller ones in the lab. Pressure serves to obtain the high temperatures necessary to quickly kill microorganisms. Specific temperatures must be obtained to ensure the microbicidal activity. The two common steam-sterilizing temperatures are 121°C

(250°F) and 132°C (270°F). These temperatures must be maintained for a minimal time to kill microorganisms, three- and one-half minutes. The stripped, sterilization tape indicators turn black as well as a biological indicator (BI) within the pack as backup. A biological indicator provides information on whether necessary conditions were met to kill a specified number of microorganisms for a given sterilization process, providing a level of confidence in the process. Endospores, or bacterial spores, are the microorganisms primarily used in BIs. They are considered some of the toughest ones to kill.

OSHA defines contaminated laundry as laundry which has been soiled with blood or other potentially infectious materials. Autoclaves demand daily attention by the staff and monthly, and yearly by the manufacturer. An immediate-use sterilizer is typically needed near an operating room and may only need to process one to three trays of instruments at a time. Most healthcare facilities, however, have large autoclave machines in their Central Supply which can process fifteen to twenty trays of instruments per cycle or even up to 625 pounds of instruments per cycle depending on size. STERIS is a leading provider of infection prevention and other products and services.

Paula, with short blond hair, is an attractive forty-eight-year-old white bespectacled female wearing baggy scrubs, no makeup ever, and is the all-business leader in Central Supply. She's not someone to mess with and keeps a tight schedule. A navy veteran, she has been heading Central Supply for four uneventful years. In fact, at a recent awards ceremony, she received an award of excellence, recognizing her leadership in her department. She has a staff of three technicians employed by the VH and appropriately trained. The Central Service Technician (CST) or Central Sterile Technician is responsible for decontaminating, sterilizing, assembling, storing, and distributing medical devices and equipment needed for patient care, especially during surgery. Hours of operation from 6:00 a.m. to 6:00 p.m. These technicians are not routinely on the call schedule. There have been some exceptions with cases extending beyond 6:00 p.m. After 6:00 p.m., the OR call team is responsible for Central Supply.

As per the next days' surgical schedule, instrument packs were picked: instruments placed on a rolled towel, a BI placed and the packs appropriately folded, non-sterile tape as the finishing touch and then autoclaved. At the close of the day, the variously identified sterilized packs were placed on the long silver metal back table adjacent to room 1. (Believe it or not, years ago, thievery in the CS and OR was a constant problem. As a result, only a select few persons were entrusted with card keys as needed for access during evenings and weekends.) Paula has been at the VH four years. At the age of forty-two, Paula had retired from the Navy Nurse Corps. Paula had a difficult transition to her current position.

Denice Saunders preceded Paula as head of Central Supply (CS). Denice had been with the VH three years and in charge of Central Supply for two years when at twenty-eight, she became pregnant. The fact that she was not married was not a great issue. The pregnancy, as it unfolded, was a great issue. *Morning sickness* lasts several weeks, but into the second trimester, it is likely to be hyperemesis gravidarum. (HG is persistent severe vomiting leading to weight loss and dehydration, as a condition occurring during pregnancy.) This can have significant effects on the mother and the baby. Denice developed hyperemesis gravidarum early in the pregnancy, having to be hospitalized on several occasions because of dehydration and malnutrition, requiring an IV port for nourishment, which became infected and had to be removed. Instead, a PICC line was inserted which she tolerated well. She continued with nausea and vomiting, became anorectic, and her ravaged poor body was in and out of the hospital for months, requiring total parenteral nutrition. She looked like the poster child for HG. Paula was asked to take on the responsibility, and she agreed, becoming the head of CS out of necessity since previously she was a floor nurse.

When Denice was finally restored back to good health, the baby was two years old. Denice had married, changed her name to Barbara Lee Dorian, taken a medical records technician course, and was hired back by the VH. She took a position in Medical Records. She was not a happy soul, for this was a huge demotion, salary-wise. She was not trying to hide but wished she could...hide. But that was four years ago, and since she has been gradually promoted to the position of director of the Medical Records Department. (Appropriate card keys were needed for chart access evenings and weekends. Obviously, the hospital was a shell of its former self.) Denice ruminates over the past. She felt that she was doing a great job as head of Central Supply, and when she had recovered, she should have been reassigned to her former job. She thinks about that every day as she reports to duty, and it wasn't just that her salary had been much higher than now. No, it had to do with prestige of all things. One, you would think, carries with it just as much hard work and is just as responsible for patient care. Lives could be lost if Central Supply made a grave (no pun intended) error with the sterilization process while Medical Records Department might be referred to as just paper shuffling, but the truth is both departments are crucial to the operations of the Veterans Hospital or any hospital.

Austin Harper was a first-class petty officer surgical technician. He had been assigned to this VH just two years ago. He was nineteen years in the navy with acceptable but not particularly glowing evaluations during his career. He once was called down for not saluting a lieutenant, a very pompous one who made a big issue of it. Austin was a divorced man with one child, a daughter who was to graduate college, and Austin had asked to attend the ceremony in another state. Initially he was granted the time off, leave. He believed that he was given that weekend off, but at the last moment, the schedule was changed, and the weekend liberty cancelled. The question was, did he know the liberty/leave had been rescinded? He had already begun his trip. He was absent from Friday afternoon returning Sunday late. Although certainly consciously, he believed that he had someone covering for him, he was mistaken. Upon his return, the blame for his absence was totally placed upon his sagging shoulders. During wartime, punishment depends upon the severity of the offense and at the discretion of the commanding officer but often includes forfeiture of pay and confinement. For instance, being AWOL for less than three days can result in a maximum penalty of confinement for one month and forfeiture of two-thirds pay for one month. After thirty days or more, service members face dishonorable discharge, forfeiture of all pay and allowances, and a one-year confinement. (These stiff rules applied in wartime but when was America not involved in war or *conflict*?)

Austin was in deep trouble. At that time, he had been a chief petty officer in charge of a small surgical suite with three operating rooms. Talk about responsibility and prestige, Austin had it. Part of his punishment was demotion to a first-class petty officer in charge of nothing and receiving transfer orders. His every two-week paycheck reminded him of this unfortunate situation. He had no support outside of the military, and his plans for retirement were put on hold. He could not live on the outside with what his pay had dropped too. Austin was a tremendously bitter man. (They were lenient!) His job was to pass instruments to the surgeons and putting up with their superiority over him. Everyone knew what had brought him to this new assignment. He was bitter, belittled, and developing a case of self-hatred. Back to wearing the bell-bottom pants and stupid hat, but he had too many years invested in the service and was stuck—all very demoralizing. There was one particularly pompous surgeon he hated to have to scrub for. He knew his job well, and in the operating room, Austin showed his best side. This surgeon literally threw instruments on the floor (which had to hit the wall first) and berated Austin every chance he had. He never had a kind word or a thank you. If the right instrument were not given to him, it would end up on the floor and a stern look of impatience to Austin. This was rocket fuel for Austin, and he did not know how to use it. They used to call that road rage on the highways. Something brewing?

Austin has made many mistakes, and some he would well remember, etched into his mind. For instance, one Friday evening after work, a group from Central Supply and the OR visited the local pub. Something he had not done previously and later wished he had not. Paula, unusual for her as well, went along with a couple of her OR friends and had one glass of wine to be sociable. The effects of the wine led Austin and Paula to a conversational friendship. Austin was a pest and wanted to date Paula. Paula did not want any relationship, and at her insistence, he stopped asking. Austin's feelings once again boiled, but there was nothing to be said. Suck it up, Austin! Why was she pushing him away from any kind of relationship, even a platonic one, just friends? Paula's schedule included having Wednesday afternoons off. She told Austin that she was avoiding having to deal with "hump day." One Wednesday, when he had the day off, he came to the hospital to see her, and she had to remind him Wednesdays were off-limits! She never took call or rotated as nursing supervisor on Wednesday nights for as long as Austin could remember and did not work on Sundays so that she could attend religious services at the Baptist Church nearby. Her upbringing included significant church involvement on Sunday mornings, church and Sunday school.

At the ceremony where Paula received her commendation, Austin attended, sitting well in the back of the room. Wine, again speaking for him, led to Austin whispering some jilted, derogatory remarks about her weight, that she was just a plain Jane who happened to be slightly heavy. His whispers were a bit too loud and overheard and got back to Paula. Unfortunately, their jobs put them in proximity, and they would bump into each other more often than they desired, an extremely uncomfortable time for Austin to have his advances turned down, even for a platonic relationship. He had never suggested that he desired anything more than just a friendship. He professed guilt for his remarks and asked for forgiveness. It never came about.

Also occurring around six months ago, an OR nurse, April Barth, was helping cleanup of the rooms at the end of the day when she screamed in pain while dealing with the dirty laundry. She had moved her gloved hands in a sweeping motion gathering contaminated drapes and gowns and was devastated when her left palm was stuck by a needle attached to a syringe that had blood-tinged fluid in it. The needle tore the glove she was wearing. The needle of the syringe had to be pulled out of the palm of her left hand. This needle and syringe was quickly disposed of. As we are creatures of habit, we try to get rid of contaminated needles and syringes quickly and naturally toss in the box for contaminated items. Two patients with relatively minor procedures under local anesthesia and a standby anesthetist had been in that room. The HIV status of the two patients from that room was not immediately known. This was about a year and a half after Austin came on board the VH. They had a one-night stand date. This same nurse was known to be promiscuous with multiple consorts…no surprise to anyone in the department, except Austin! Another bust he was to find out. When the nurse reported the needlestick, the news went ballistic. Of course, with the laboratory tests required, she also found out that she was six weeks pregnant. Post-exposure prophylaxis (PEP) is the use of antiretroviral drugs, tenofovir, and emtricitabine after a single high-risk event to stop HIV seroconversion. PEP must be started as soon as possible to be effective—and always within seventy-two hours of a possible exposure. These drugs were known to have teratogenic effects.

What about the pregnancy? April had spoken to Austin, letting him know that likely he was not the biological father of the baby. Blood drawn on the two patients in question were negative for HIV. Four months into the pregnancy, April went into labor, and came to the emergency room. There, she delivered a baby that was grossly deformed with multiple congenital defects, stillborn. She was not allowed to see the baby, it being so grotesque. The baby had anencephaly, which is the absence of a major portion of the brain, skull, and scalp that occurs during embryonic development. It is a cephalic disorder that results from a neural tube defect that occurs when the rostral (head) end of the neural tube fails to close, usually between the twenty-third and twenty-sixth day following conception. Strictly speaking, the Greek term translates as "without head." She was observed for a couple of hours, and there was no bleeding, the placenta small and intact. (Photos of the baby were taken in the emergency room to be placed in her record.) She refused a D&C, was discharged, and given a two-week liberty to recover. Emotionally, she would probably never recover. She was able to return to work and had a great deal of support from all her coworkers. She was reassigned to a non-patient care capacity until follow-up HIV status proved negative. Then she could return to her old position in the OR. She was truly fortunate to have a job to return to.

This had all occurred six months before the upheaval of that Monday OR crash.

One of the startling findings when the VH and the teaching hospital communicated was that the transferred patients abscesses all grew the same bacteria. Proving that somewhere, somehow all these patients were infected from the same source. This, indeed, was not an accident. Infectious disease committees pooled their resources at the teaching hospital, which included Dr. Friedman of infectious diseases. Dr. John Jones directed the Infection Committee at the VH and the CDC also in touch regarding progress of the investigation. Now the investigation had to come up with a source before it happened again.

4

One of the very first actions of Dr. Dick Fischer when he took the job as administrator of the teaching hospital was to look for what he referred to as "step-down space," more like an extended care facility. He did not have far to search but back to the nursing home facility associated with the defunct community hospital. As you will recall, when community hospital had its last breath, so did the nursing facility adjacent to it. It took some time to get the remaining patients to proper facilities, a few cases a two-hour drive from their family, unfortunately. The hospital closed its doors in 2013, and by 2015, the nursing facility followed suit, so when Dick looked at the facility in 2026, it appeared that the building would be a possibility. Originally it was a 150-bed facility. It took two years to refurbish this spinoff campus, but it was accomplished and easily staffed. Some of the personnel of that facility were still in New Fledgling and were rehired after some refresher courses taken at the teaching hospital and with updating of their credentials where needed. It began as a seventy-five-bed unit. It had new life; its pulse restored even better than it ever had been.

The facility also had become a teaching venue, another opportunity for residents and students to learn about geriatrics and the diseases that result in nursing home placement. Just because an elderly patient was transferred to the nursing home did not absolve their *teaching* of geriatric illnesses and even learning about something not taught on medical campuses, the art, and the physiology and psychology of the dying process. Psychology courses as an undergraduate and learning the works of pioneers such as Elisabeth Kübler-Ross on *Death and Dying* is taught prior to medical school but only if one has taken courses regarding same, like psychology, always trying to find ways to make that experience one to not be indifferent to (dying and taxes). There is, unfortunately, little one learns about death and the dying process outside of hospice care and serious patient care would be one on one so not larger than a couple of individuals at a time, an elective six weeks at the hospice in Fullerton just thirty miles from the campus. So now perhaps much can be learned by the affiliation of nursing homes with medical college and residency programs. One or two students at a time to begin with. Pioneering again!

Of course, Dr. Rexford Swiss was delighted when first hearing of the project, glad to be back in his element treating the often deadly bedsores—also called pressure ulcers and decubitus ulcers—injuries to skin and underlying tissue resulting from prolonged pressure on the skin from hard surfaces. The surface doesn't have to be hard, just enough to exceed venous pressure. Bedsores most often develop on skin that covers bony areas of the body, such as the heels, ankles, hips, and tailbone. People most at risk of bedsores have medical conditions that limit their ability to change positions or cause them to spend most of their time in a bed or chair. These were avoided only by constant attention. Breakdown of skin from shearing forces, particularly when the patient tends to slide from the upright position, quite often is a mechanism to have to deal with.

Bedsores can develop over hours or days. Most sores heal with treatment, but many never heal completely. You can take steps to help prevent bedsores and help them heal. High degrees of sepsis are associated and often the primary cause of death…infection. (This was what took the life of Superman in 2004, and it was worse than kryptonite. In 1995, he became paralyzed from the neck down following a horse-riding accident. He founded the Christopher Reeve Paralysis Foundation in 1998 to promote research on spinal cord injuries. He developed sepsis from a sacral decubitus after a lengthy stay in the chair for a family's event leading to his death.)

The age-old decubitus ulcer. They will always be with us: the older the patient, the level of care, and the ability to move around normally or not at all whether it is in a facility or at home. They often would be simply neglected. You almost always hear the term *benign neglect* when that really was not benign. Often the caregivers really cared, but it was a function of time and not necessarily training. That would require a weekend course to be trained in wound care, and Dr. Swiss was quite willing to show the nurses all that they needed to know, himself board-certified in that specialty. Most were treated with wet to dry saline dressings. When dry and carefully removed, it debrides the ulceration. That and off-loading are simple, and occasionally when the ulceration has been adequately prepared, surgical procedures can cover these wounds. KISS (keep it simple, stupid). No, the problem is time, not enough time to turn twenty-plus patients every two hours, to off-load soft tissue off hard surfaces. Many of these patients had lost weight and were malnourished; they were skin and bone.

The renovated, resurrected facility was still going strong, and its presence was great for the community. Tender loving care could also be learned and given there. Med students and residents were each challenged to keep their patients free of this awful situation—turn from side to side every two hours around the clock. Impossible? A serial way of judging how things are going was a weekly conference complete with a slide show. It would be a feather in the cap of those with good progress. Every patient with a wound was discussed in conference where exchange of ideas could be done. Photos of these ulcerations are a nice way of documenting progress.

Its well-known and advertised ad nauseam on the cable networks inviting watchers to call the attorney if ever you have had thus and so operation that did not go perfectly well, drug complication, or decubitus ulcer in a loved one, even a fall. Lawyers are camped somewhere outside the hospitals (sic) and particularly nursing homes to learn of that fall, that bedsore; they are right on top of it, or they hear from their operatives within every facility (and they existed, and for a price, these people would turn their mother or best friend over to an attorney. Father, forgive me). The last time doctors and lawyers worked together was to have Roe v Wade be a household name, allowing legalized abortion in America. A work of Satan. As it worked its way, through subsequent court cases, by 2020, abortion was legal up even to the point the baby's head engaged in the birth canal. After 2020, when the democrats took power over the country, never releasing it back to reality, taxpayers subsidized roughly 24 percent of all abortion costs in the US with 6.6 percent borne by federal taxpayers and the remaining 17.4 percent picked up by state taxpayers. If we apply the 24 percent figure to the total number of abortions, this is equivalent to taxpayers paying the full cost of 250,000 abortions a year, with about $70,000 financed by federal taxpayers and $80,000 financed by state taxpayers (https://www.forbes.com/sites/theapothecary/2015/10/02/are-american-taxpayers-paying-for-abortion/?sh=7a57380d6a4b).

When reality settled in and thanks to a conservative SCOTUS and finally a true conservative, charismatic, no-nonsense leader (deliverer) in the late 2030's, there was hope that God still loved his people.

One of the cases at the nursing facility that haunted Dr. Swiss involved a thirty-seven-year-old paraplegic man who had been the victim of a motorcycle accident nearly twenty years prior. He had been fed with different diets and procedures for feeding tubes of one kind or another over the years. He essentially had no close family or representative. He could speak in an understandable manner and was very cooperative. He had never had any bedsores and was really considered extremely fortunate and appreciative. His last gastrostomy tube had been used, but for months, there had been the leakage of gastric juice around the tube. The tube had fallen out with the result of constant bile and gastric acid drainage onto the skin. It is interesting that the nurses would put a few 4x4s over the opening in the upper abdomen, and within minutes, the dressings would be saturated with bile. There was a 4x4-inch bright-red excoriated wound. For the time being (he was a DNR), he was nourished intravenously by way of a PIC line (peripheral intravenous catheter). Dr. Swiss talked it over with the patient at length, that he had a gastrocutaneous fistula. What he needed, it was felt, was an operation to close the fistula. He was becoming more malnourished by the day.

Surgically, he did well. An anesthetist on the case sedated him mildly. After using local anesthesia, a small incision adjacent to the fistula was made, and under direct vision, a surgical stapler was placed across the fistula and fired. No problem at that point. The incision and fistula site healed well. The rash disappeared. The problem was that Dr. Swiss had admittedly overestimated the patient's ability to breathe deeply. It began with a fever of 102, and chest x-ray revealed pneumonia. Malnutrition, inability to cough or breathe deeply, he was headed for a ventilator to augment his breathing. He could not be placed on a ventilator as per his pre-op wishes, so he became septic from the bilateral pneumonia, lingered awake for a time, and died about ten days later. Dr. Swiss had shared his faith with this man.

The only thing remaining in his room, on the bedside table was one of those red postage-sized booklets about the four spiritual laws to salvation. It was as if he was being told by the young man that all was well with his soul.

5

When Dr. Alex Martin's wife Sally divorced him, their two boys were barely two and three years old. That was the Alex of old. Now he is a different creature who loved the Lord and loved Hannah, status post soul and heart transplant having the beating of his own son's heart in his chest, a constant reminder. He cannot help but thank their God for the sacrifice. They remained optimistic regarding his heart. Those two boys were now eight and nine years old. Their mother was truly kind to let the boys have some time with their father after his transplant. She was impressed in the change that had come over her former husband. She had remarried just two years after her divorce, and her husband was not interested in adopting the boys or changing their last name. He had been a Jehovah's Witness most of his life and was set on the two boys being indoctrinated into the same faith. Sally had married Fred Storz, having dated only a short time, but his faith was not shared by the boys' mother. In her discussions regarding Alex and Hannah adopting the boys, she prayed that they would steer them away from what was felt to be a cult.

Professor or doctor, he likes to be called Dad or Alex. It's Thanksgiving, that time of the year when the family has so much to be thankful for. God's Son gave his life for the salvation of the world; Alex's son Sammy, thirty-two years old, had led Alex to a relationship with the Lord a couple of days before his death, giving his heart to his father, and then he died. It is strange to have a part of you that is not really a part of you. I wonder if there is a communal sense one has after a transplant, especially of the heart, for it reminds one every second that it is in us just as our salvation, and the Holy Spirit reminds us of whose we are. You might be grateful for a time, but it passes; we forget how we were before, and we perhaps cringe. Alex believes in his heart (his son's heart) that he belongs to God, that for the past two years, he has been a new creature; the old is died, behold the new. These two years have seen a change relationally with former friends, colleagues, and peers. Alex is a living testimony of the existence of God. Those on the list from which they send out Christmas cards, the closest to seem to have abandoned him. They pretend that the Jesus freak no longer exists. They do not want to associate with Alex and Hannah and the two young adult boys/men. It is a sad feeling, and yet to be the Lord's is a joyful feeling. Anyone who will sit with him for a period of just moments to hours will know that this is not the Alex of the past. They know, they just do not want to spend any time with such a changed life. To some associates, it is an embarrassment. It is as though Alex has leprosy or was a werewolf; you just need a silver bullet or the crucifix, and they will run and not walk away. They don't like the sight of you because you remind them of who made the change, and you must vote with your heart and soul one way or the other.

After Sally Martin divorced Alex, he didn't look back, for he was headed for the top as the biologist of the century or at least of the Catholic Church. After a truly short, confusing courtship, Sally, a year or so later, married Fred Storz who belonged to the Jehovah's Witness faith. She was clueless early on as to what this religion was all about. The boys, James and John Martin, were four and five years old. Sally protected her boys, not allowing them to participate in what she believes was a cult. Storz backed off until Sally became desperately ill from ovarian cancer. Storz himself was a disillusioned JW and wanted out. Once in the faith, you do not just walk away, and if you do so, you are *shunned* by all your Witness friends and especially by family members in the faith. You are essentially dead.

(After the FDA alerted Johnson & Johnson in October 2019 of the results showing asbestos in their container of baby powder, the healthcare giant reacted by issuing a voluntary recall of lot #22318RB, which included thirty-three containers. Johnson & Johnson stated this was done "out of an abundance of caution," and rightly so as the FDA has said, "There are no known safe levels of asbestos." According to Reuters, some major US retailers have followed a similar course of action and removed all twenty-two-ounce containers from their shelves. Nevertheless, it did not take long for Johnson & Johnson to reconsider their situation and make another decision. On May 19, 2020, Johnson & Johnson decided to stop the sale of talc-based baby powder in the United States and Canada, a decision probably motivated by the thousands of lawsuits pending before a US District Court in New Jersey, claiming that talc caused their mesothelioma and ovarian cancer.)

Sally Martin had been ill for over a year with rather nonspecific symptoms: abdominal bloating or swelling, suddenly feeling a full sensation when eating, anorexic, losing weight, discomfort in the lower abdomen, and change in bowel habits like constipation and frequent need to urinate. She saw a nurse practitioner who ordered an ultrasound study of the abdomen and pelvis, and one ovary appeared enlarged, and there was free fluid in the abdomen and pelvis. She was referred to gynecology and Dr. Suzanne Grayson. Laparoscopically it appeared that both ovaries were involved with tumor (positive intraoperative confirmation by pathology), and Sally not wanting more children, Grayson did a pelvic sweep, removing both ovaries and the uterus and sending free abdominal fluid for evaluation. There were *seeds* of tumor cells on the diaphragm and other organs. She would need further treatment with chemotherapy with at least a stage 3 ovarian cancer and a prognosis for five-year survival at 49 percent.

The class action suit regarding Johnson & Johnson's baby powder of the 2020s still had some fire in it, and when first ill, Sally had seen the advertised class action suit attorneys and had a contract with them. With the help of an attorney, the moneys received were to be put into a trust account for the boys to be made available to them after they turned twenty-five. Sally wanted to give the boys a chance to make it on their own into their early twenties. Sally's Will specifically designated any monies received from the class action suit was to be placed in the boys' trust account.

Who would take care of her children? Alex was their true biological father, and since her husband Fred was a staunch JW, try as he might, their mother would not allow them to participate in the cult. Therefore, Fred was not particularly close to the boys, and even though he was a kind person, he would not force them into the faith. Sally did not follow her husband's faith. Sally had discussed the children with Hannah and Alex years ago. Now they felt that the Lord was leading them to adopt the boys and take care of them. They still had some growing up to do. Hannah and Alex were not married but had to strongly consider marriage. They did love each other. So… Pastor Nash performed their wedding ceremony.

The boys moved in with these godly parents and would do well in years to come with Alex and Hannah guiding James and John away from the JW faith. Nevertheless, the kids, though young, had been indoctrinated the year Sally was sick. They both underwent the JW baptismal rite, and accordingly they were under the rulings of the cult forever. Sally could do little to influence them; otherwise, she was so terribly ill. Until they were under the roof of Hannah and Alex, Fred did his best raising the kids as JWs: coloring-in exercises, sing-along sessions and hours of door-to-door preaching. They were like magnets to the faith. Alex and Hannah had a tough time breaking that attraction. Fred remained a kind father showing no untoward emotions, no anger, and no hostility only sadness for himself, but he himself had an awakening after the boys were with their real parents. He wanted out, but you do not just walk away from the faith. The *shunning* is a deep measure when no one will associate with one after their awakening. Many who want out are afraid of the repercussions, so they do what is referred to as "fading away," which is a baby step at a time over a year or more. If they are discovered of doing this and try to leave, they go through visible *disfellowshipping.* Decorating a Christmas tree, if discovered, could lead to disfellowshipping for five years!

Fred Storz had been raised in a JW family. Most people think "no blood transfusions" when they think about the JW, but there is so much more. He was taught not to celebrate any holidays—Easter, Christmas, Fourth of July—no saluting of the flag, no wearing of a cross, and no birthday celebration. Fred's parents were elderly JW members and sensed that Fred wanted out. They warned Fred that what he was doing was only going to cause awful consequences from shunning.

The Jehovah's Witness religion has the highest turnover rate. Some two thirds of its members leave. The leadership excessively controls its members. If one desires to leave the JW faith, they are *shunned* by its membership. They leave all their family members and friends and are shunned by them strongly so that it is a hard decision to leave, for then you would no longer have any friends or family for that matter.

The JW faith might be referred to as "living in a bubble." Outside of that religious bubble is only darkness leading some to embrace escape only to find on the outside, a deep depression not unlike post-traumatic stress disorder and, in many cases, leading to suicide. They find themselves regretting their *awakening*. Guilt keeps many enslaved to the JW. Sally had been a great influence keeping her boys from becoming trapped by the cult, but the kids were not home free.

The bottom line with regards to the Jehovah's Witness faith, one has a dilemma at the door when the doorbell rings and the *preaching* begins.

Most persons will use a slammed door technique or a flame-thrower attitude at the cultist. As a Christian, we have a commandment to preach the Good News to all who come our way. First Peter 3:15 says always being ready! You can choose to slam the door or engage the visitor with kindness. Know what you believe and be ready, which takes study and certainly being interested in the fate of their souls. When confronted in kindness after they raise a scripture, one should try to get them to come back another time, giving you time to prepare what to do with them and not to frighten them to not return. The Holy Spirit is in charge at this point. Prayer! They are not allowed to wear a cross, a form of idolatry. Every so often they ready their parishioners for the apocalypse, the end of time, and they obviously have been wrong at this point, several times in fact. Remember each member is a person before being a witness.

You will recall that when Paul traveled to Athens, he saw the statue pointed out as "the unknown God." On Mars Hill, he kindly and respectfully explained his point of view. He did not bowl them over which left it open for them to think more about his words and even with some of the Athenians. This is more notable that some believed, some interested to seek out Paul for further discussions.

The teachings of the Jehovah's Witness church is abstinence from receiving blood transfusions, and that is about all a non-witness knows about the faith. The Bible verse, "You are to abstain from… blood." While blood loss is a risk of transplant surgery, some doctors do not view patient refusal of blood transfusion as a major transplant risk. The first publicized case of transplantation of a Jehovah's Witness appeared in the mid-1980s from the UCLA heart transplant team. Since then, numerous other cases (cadaveric and living donor) have been published, including kidney and pancreas and lung and liver. For those with the best blood management skills, transplant can indeed be a viable course; however, optimal blood management before and during surgery are no big deal, but in the remaining third, the procedure after receiving a successful bloodless-transplant period, the patient has received his/her organ, and done well yet, the potential for clinical need of blood transfusion remains.

There may be post success bleeding of a significate amount, and that becomes a real issue, necessary lifesaving blood transfusion may be critical to the survival of the transplanted JW patient. Red blood cells transport oxygen. Our kidneys are oxygen sensors. When they detect an oxygen shortage in the blood, they activate the production of EPO (erythropoietin), and the level of EPO in the blood may rise as much as a thousandfold. The EPO stimulates the bone marrow to produce more red blood cells, which in turn transport more oxygen.

6

Kidneys are organs that filter waste products from the blood. They are also involved in regulating blood pressure, electrolyte balance, and red blood cell production in the body. Symptoms of kidney failure are due to the buildup of waste products and excess fluid in the body that may cause weakness, shortness of breath, lethargy, swelling, and confusion. James's has known chronic kidney disease, CKD. Early on, there were no specific symptoms.

There are numerous causes of kidney failure, and treatment of the underlying disease may be the first step in correcting the kidney abnormality. Treatment of the underlying cause of kidney failure may return kidney function to normal. Lifelong efforts to control blood pressure and diabetes may be the best way to prevent chronic kidney disease and its progression to kidney failure.

James has been followed for several months by a nephrologist and a transplant team. This all began slowly. James loved sports, and when asked to play catch with his brother, he balked. He was just laying around watching television. James was a devoted Seahawk fan, and when they were scheduled for a night game, James was not interested in staying up that late. He was a snackaholic, now not interested in eating. Sally noticed James's ankles were swollen, and he seemed short-winded. Sally, poorly feeling herself, took James to his pediatrician, and the doctor was very alarmed. He explained the abnormalities in the blood work and that there was fluid in his lungs. His potassium and calcium levels were abnormal, dangerously abnormal which could affect the heart's electronics.

With medical management, James began to improve. He had been added to the list of waiting for a kidney and joyfully was removed from that horrible waiting list. All were thrilled when James became hungry again and was playing catch with his brother. Medical management was continued, lab abnormalities improved, and the doctors amazed. Was this going to be just a temporary respite? Can a teenager ask his brother to give him one of his kidneys? It has been done many, many times, but hopefully Brother John is off the hook, but he would gladly, if needed in the future, donate a kidney for his brother. On subsequent visits to the nephrologist, James continued to make steady improvement. Miraculous? Sally, nearing the end, was still alive while this was going on, and she seemed to wait until James was declared on the mend.

James has been doing well as far as activity level goes and really without complaint. The doctors, keeping tabs on James, were always anxious when Hannah called. They had alerted her early on that his kidneys were not functioning at 100 percent. He has been doing well in his schoolwork, keeping up with classmates. One interesting thing they did every year at home was to mark the heights of the children standing them up against the wall. Though only a year apart in age, there seemed to be separation between the two a little more each year by height. Of course, one of the signs in children with chronic kidney disease is their stature—that is a failure to thrive. So the boys were not close at all in their height. Growth failure is a complication of chronic kidney disease in which children do not grow as expected. When a child is below the third percentile—meaning 97 percent of children the same age and gender are taller—he or she has growth failure. CKD is kidney disease that does not go away with treatment and tends to get worse over time. Alex and Hannah understood and became more worried when James's started lounging around and sleeping and not eating. Mom always was checking James's feet for swelling, and they were swollen. He was not peeing as much either. Hannah wasted no time and took him to the nephrologist where clinically, as well as chemistry profile, got him a trip to the hospital.

Rather suddenly James, fourteen, had developed acute renal failure and required emergency hemodialysis. His degree of CKD up to this point was just a talking point about the future. Alex and Hannah were anticipating someday he might need dialysis. They trusted all the staff who had explained the procedure to them. The kidneys not working, lab abnormalities were becoming worse by the day. Since hemodialysis was needed urgently, there needed to be a large vessel to send the boy's blood through the filtering system. Without dialysis, prognosis for this rapid disease state is not good, and mortality is high. The two acute procedures were night and day. A fistula, joining an artery and vein which over time would create the sizable vessel, unfortunately takes weeks to mature for use. Too late for James!

He would need the placement of a catheter, a Vas Cath. This double-lumen catheter is the standard for accessing the dialysis machine in an acute situation. Although rather frightening, the gentle staff and mom holding James's hand, they proceeded. The catheter really is painless because local anesthesia is infiltrated under the clavicle, and after assuring, the local anesthesia was working the firm, but flexible catheter was placed after which James said, "When are you going to start putting in the needle?" He never felt a thing. When assured that the catheter was in the right position by a chest x-ray and there were no complications, they were connected to the dialysis machine, and the machine right away had James's blood circulating and being purified. James tolerated this all very well. Laboratory data showed good results. But the ultimate treatment would require a kidney transplant.

Brother John was becoming ill himself which eliminated him from donating one of his kidneys to his brother. He was undergoing an anemia workup. The situation was getting out of control. Hannah volunteered to donate one of her kidneys. Unfortunately, after the massive blood transfusions needed to save her life in 2008, there seemed to be a matching problem eliminating her as a donor.

Alex had done extremely well status post heart transplant. His blood work, an ideal match for donating a kidney to James. Had situations like this occurred with any frequency? Rare to have a HT patient donate a kidney, but this was looking like a lifesaving situation. With James becoming desperately ill, kidney transplant was his only salvation. The JW baptism the boys received brought up the question of blood transfusion possibly necessary. But this family was incredibly special, and the ties between the brothers and the JW had faded such that they didn't care what the JW faith would mandate regarding receiving blood. So it was that Alex, a stable HT patient, would be his son's kidney donor.

Dr. Samantha Rodgers was no stranger to this family. Alex was near death because of pump failure just a couple of years ago due to hypertensive cardiomyopathy. Samantha had been the transplant surgeon placing Alex son's heart into a dying Alex's empty chest. Now "Dr. Sam" and her team of fellows would be the transplant team which would be doing the procedure on a teenager using a spare kidney from his heart transplanted dad. Rare but there are similar cases in the literature, successful ones which was very encouraging.

Since last we saw Dr. Sam, there have been some notable changes in her life. Of course, she has become director of the Transplant Institute, a laudable achievement with not that large an amount of experience, but she has proven herself time and again. She also had fallen in love with one of the fellows in the program, and they are now married. When confronted acutely regarding James Martin needing a kidney ASAP, she searched the literature and found only a handful of cases of father to son kidney transplants but really found none of this nature, the father having had a heart transplant. This perhaps would be a reportable case for the literature. That, of course, the father's transplanted heart was from James older brother Samuel whom he had never met except that his heart was now beating strongly and benignly in the father's chest.

Hannah, James's mom, had been liaison in the Transplant Institute for some time. She now became just a worried wife and mother sitting in the post-op area holding her breath while in one operating room, Sam's fellow (husband) was doing the donor kidney while Sam was now doing the recipient. It read like the script from a soap opera! And all went well on both ends. Recovery was successful, and James was now off dialysis with normalizing renal function.

The Watch Tower Society is the voice of truth for today for the Jehovah's Witness. Challenging the Watch Tower is equal to challenging God's authority, an intolerable offence which can lead to the possibility of shunning. Their information all comes from what the society holds. Reading any apostate literature is as bad as watching pornographic *literature*. Personally, one should approach them with the love of Jesus. Flat-out arguing with a JW is a mistake. God's Holy Spirit led them to your front door for his purpose. The worse that you can do is claim to be a believer and to treat them like you are not. One of the worst things is to be referred to as a "phony Christian." What is worse though is really being a phony Christian, a pretender. One may claim that they are Christians but carnal at best.

The drivers of the Northside Laundry Service vans were Warren Day and Russell Sanders. Warren swiped his key card to gain entrance to the back door of the Central Supply Department. He had very much looked forward to visits to the Veterans Hospital which usually were scheduled for Tuesdays, Thursdays, and Sundays. This thirty-six-year-old Muslim American had been involved with this laundry service for only three years. Russell Sanders fifty-year-old white male covered the other days. They both covered territories north and west of New Fledgling. Over those three years, Warren had enjoyed spending time getting to know Paula at the VH. Initially on his visits, he brought in the clean linens and then gathered the tan-white bags of soiled linens and would say hello to Paula and very slowly over those three years little by little. A compliment here and there, he began seeing Paula as a friend and not just a client.

His interest in Paula was overshadowed by his wide-eyed attention to how things were carried out in her department. He learned the basics of sterilization, the care of instruments, and how packs were put together and autoclaved. He asked about the "menu cards" taped to the walls of the department above the countertop. He was showing so much interest. Paula shared quite a bit of the goings-on in the department with him. He was briefed on the fail-safe sterilization process with the changing of the tape to black and the sterility insert in the packs proving sterility.

Warren and Paula occasionally would have a coffee break together. There was a significant age gap. On one of these occasions, the date topic came up by Warren. Paula felt that Warren was getting too close, and she told him, in no uncertain terms, that she did not like his pushing to have a relationship, that Warren would just do his job and let her do hers. An emotional implosion for Warren. He was sickened by this rejection, kind of the straw which broke the camel's back. He thought that he was through with rejections because of his race, being that of a Muslim American.

There were times particularly on a quiet Sunday, Warren and Russell would make deliveries to the VH together, and Warren would point out what he had learned of the sterilization process, of the care of the instruments, and how things were sterilized and the failsafe method of determining sterility.

The Medical College of San Petra was having their third-year clerks rotate through the Central Supply/interface with the surgical suite to help in the VH, a relatively short six-week rotation. After that rotation, they were experienced enough that if it be in their future and they had to setup a rural hospital's Central Supply Department or at least monitor it, they would be able to do that. It is not unusual for a program to rotate students and residents through off-site facilities like the VH. There are rotations through pediatrics at Children's Hospital some forty miles away as well as through large gyn facilities at a distance.

Aaryan "Erin" Abdalla, the third-year surgical clerk, is rotating through Central Supply and surgery and has been for two weeks now. Enjoying learning, Aaryan was a first-generation Muslim American, a very bright well-liked twenty-six-year-old man.

7

Patrick Poley was a forty-two years old AA male Army infantry veteran who, after two tours of duty in Afghanistan and withdrawal finally from the Middle East never-ending war, has been troubled for several years since with a persistent perirectal abscess with drainage off and on. He had it drained while in the Middle East ten years ago.

Sergeant Poley was six feet two and has been gaining weight over the past several years and weighs about 240 pounds. Practically every week, Patrick had foul-smelling drainage from his bottom on his underwear. He showered every other day and let the water hit that area, but it was simply too difficult logistically to get into anything like the whirlpool, and he had no bathtub. After the drainage procedure so many years ago, he was told to take sitz baths twice a day which he has tried to do but not religious about it and not easily negotiated. Days will go by without drainage, but slowly over a week or so, the drainage returns, but the discomfort, always there to some extent, is lessened with the drainage. He is a stubborn individual, living alone, a recluse, and must wait on "the last straw" in many respects in his life. He has type 2 diabetes and is an alcoholic.

Two Saturdays ago, the sergeant gave in to that last straw from his bottom and came to the ER at the VH early that Saturday morning around 3:00 a.m. He was found to have a large horseshoe-shaped tender, erythematous, tense mass around the anus (really about the size and shape of a small horseshoe). He was in extreme pain, appearing acutely ill and had no drainage over the past two weeks which he thought was positive…his exam suggested otherwise. He also had a temperature of 102 and an elevated white blood cell count on a CBC greater than 20,000. Dr. Rogers, the chief resident in surgery, from the on-call sleeping quarters, assigned this patient to one of his interns, a young Dr. Ronald Smith, and his student to evaluate and to present the case at rounds that morning, and the lot fell to the lucky third-year clerk Aaryan (pronounced Erin) Abdalla. Dr. Rogers had not seen this patient. This patient was taken to the operating room prior to any rounds being done before being staffed with any attending.

The intern, having just graduated from medical school, without question, had jumped the gun and felt that the patient was in too much pain to be delayed and needed to be drained ASAP. Sadly, second and third opinions of the chief resident and attendings were glaringly absent because in the intern's mind, he wanted the procedure done due to the degree of the patient's pain and high fever. It would be a good case to present and would bolster his status with the staff.

Attending and residents did not have an opportunity to look at the patient preoperatively; an eye on evaluation of this man's critical problem would have perhaps saved the day. Unfortunately, half of the persons who get this will die! Neither the intern, just graduating from med school, nor the medical student (his first real clinical experience in the hospital) had ever seen an entity such as this.

The operating room call crew had been brought in that early Saturday morning, and forty-two-year-old Pat Poley was put to sleep, a cephalosporin given intravenously, and he was placed in the lithotomy (legs up) position. With the intern looking over the student's shoulder supervising, he was alarmed at what he was seeing. Suddenly, as if on cue, he was called to the emergency room, and he left the operating room. The nervous third-year student "lanced the perirectal boil" (his words at the deposition). In return, he got a cup of creamy tan pus that shot out covering the front of his gown, scaring him half to death. His *incision* was more like a puncture wound. The student irrigated the drainage site with a modicum of saline. A small Penrose drain was inserted, a bulky dressing applied. The necessary procedure was terribly botched because of no appropriate supervision. The mass looked smaller to the student. (He did not digitally explore the wound.)

The patient's temperature decreased over that day and through the night. He tolerated clear liquids, and the patient was discharged Sunday afternoon after being instructed to leave the dressing in place and told to return on Tuesday's general surgery clinic. The report from the abscess material was not on the chart when the patient came to the Tuesday clinic. The patient had been given prescriptions for Keflex and pain meds. He already had pain meds at home and a few antibiotic "capsules," so he did not get the prescriptions filled. He needed the pain medication and the antibiotic because the case was "half-assed" (no pun intended) done! There had been the necessary specimen on this case. Why wasn't there any record of it in the patient's chart? The scrub tech had placed the "cup of pus" in the specimen *room* a flap door to the pathology department. When discovered there on Monday and with no label, it was disposed of.

(That was the job of Milton Conover, sixty-year-old AA janitor/orderly who has been with the VH so many years that he has lost count. His story began long ago with his own involvement in medical education. Milton had a disabling stroke which required nearly a year to recover from through off and on physical therapy. He has always had his instructions for each department. He was an excellent employee mainly working the second floor where the intensive care units, Central Supply, and the surgery suite were located. From his stroke, Mr. Conover was left with a noticeable limp and just a smidgen of left arm weakness. He seemed to have mood swings, mainly bouts of depression which could last several weeks, and therefore, he was not a full-time employee.)

The intern, Dr. Ronald Smith, really had not supervised the student. He was called away for an emergency in the ER; a patient needed a chest tube for a collapsed lung. But the sergeant was already under anesthesia. He really should have had two radial two- to three-inch incisions, one at nine o'clock and one at three o'clock, the incisions digitally explored to break up loculate areas, irrigated with copious amounts of saline and dressing applied and perhaps a large Penrose drain to keep the incisions open!

When he did return for his appointment in the clinic, sick as a dog, the intern unfortunately had to return him to the operating room late Tuesday afternoon straight from the clinic. Dr. Smith did what he should have done in the first place with the nervous third-year medical student now looking over his shoulder this time. (Too little, too late.) Yes, there was purulent pus under pressure particularly from the three o'clock incision. He had not had proper treatment of this serious condition for years, and it did not get any better on Tuesday for no debridement was done. He was admitted to the surgical intensive care unit for wound care, twice daily sitz baths and periodic digitalization exams. No cultures had been taken because he was on antibiotics. When searched for culture reports from the Saturday drainage, none could be found. Apparently when the student did his half-assed job, he forgot to label the specimen. He was so shaken up from all the pus under pressure he omitted sending any C & S material. But there had been a specimen! A "cup of pus" without identification.

The unfortunate sergeant spiked a temp of 102.5 late that post-op night. The dressing was removed and cultures taken, but how reliable were the current wound cultures at this point? They were giving him an IV cephalosporin—totally inadequate. The situation seemed to be getting out of hand, confusing to the staff and patient who was losing consciousness falsely attributed to the effects of the anesthesia. They had painted themselves into a corner and had to go up the chain of command for further instructions. The chief resident was aghast when he finally did see the patient. Never picturing this, because of lack of experience and now with the patient in shock, he asked for a medical consult from infectious disease. Of course, the only real specialist in infectious disease in the area was Dr. Friedman, now with the teaching hospital in New Fledgling. He was asked to see the patient as soon as possible. Dr. John Jones was an Internist on the VH staff who had a special interest in infectious diseases and had two residents and two senior clerks rotating every six weeks. They were essentially the infectious disease department at the VH. They were asked to give their opinion. As it turned out, the small group with any expertise at the VH did see the patient, but they only assisted in the precode management of the sergeant.

Dr. Friedman recommended waiting for him to see the patient before ordering more antibiotics, and he would come to the VH early the next morning, Wednesday. The good sergeant did not make it through the night. Dr. Friedman did come by midmorning Wednesday, looking for the patient but finding an empty bed. No chart. Patient in the morgue after a long night with the intern and medical student and helpless internal medicine staff trying to save this patient's life.

Here is what had happened: the patient's "undrained" or "poorly drained" perirectal abscess extended into the perineum and into the skin of the scrotum. The combination of certain bacteria, spreading necrosis while the patient was complaining of worsening pain and spiking fevers. Extremely tender to touch (and frankly "extremely tender to look at"). The bacterial combination caused the necrosis and the crepitant nature of this surgical disease is air in these tissues from the different bacterial toxins.

Fournier's gangrene is typically caused by one of three to four different kinds of bacteria. The combination of bacteria damages blood vessels and produces toxins and enzymes that destroy tissue. The infection spreads along the connecting tissue plane between the skin and underlying muscles. The infection commonly starts in the area between genitals and rectum, known as the perineum, and spreads outward underneath the skin. It can also spread outside the genital area into the abdominal wall or buttocks. Proper antibiotics are critical. He had received one antibiotic, insufficient for this disease. Appropriate antibiotics certainly were needed but without properly debriding the necrosis, getting well ahead of it with perhaps multiple surgical procedures; the patient did not have a chance.

What has all this to do with our characters at the two facilities forty miles apart? Frankly, everyone is involved because of the critical nature of this disease. The chief resident should have seen the patient when he first presented. The intern did not supervise the original "drainage procedure." When reoperated on Tuesday evening, I and D was done appropriately but short of the debridement of dead and dying tissue, so extremely needed. Dr. Friedman could have been called sooner and recommended to transfer but, again, too late. How does a patient with Fournier's necrosis/gangrene effect our current situation?

All of this is temporally related to a specific time span. This near-deadly serious problem began Saturday early one weekend before the *meltdown*.

The cultures taken from the sergeant's bottom off antibiotics interestingly grew two bacteria, E. coli and MRSA, a methicillin-resistant Staphylococcus aureus. This bacterial combination was responsible for the five patients who were following the time frame. Now we have the fact before us (only missing B. frag). All related but how in the VA system could this have happened?

The sergeant's case was Saturday early in the morning. He had to be returned to the operating room the following Tuesday afternoon for proper drainage however because our intern was not aware of the disease process (nor did he make any attempt to quickly learn about it). There was no excision of dead and dying tissue allowing the disease to progress. The surrounding dying skin and soft tissue needing to be aggressively debrided, he failed again. The third-year medical student was extremely embarrassed seeing the proper method of incision and drainage. The intern was shocked to realize how progressively downhill the course had become but made no effort to take the time to research the process of this disease. At that point, he began strongly considering transfer to New Fledgling. Too late.

The VH did not realize how sick Sgt. Pat Poley was. Correctly done, they could/should have transferred while there was still time to help him. The teaching hospital would have received one sick patient needing appropriate antibiotics and aggressive debridement of spreading necrotic tissue. The words *touch and go* would apply. If the transfer had been made, a CT scan would have been done ASAP in the trauma area before placing the patient in the SICU. Air would have been seen subdermally halfway up the lateral chest wall. Vital signs deteriorating rapidly from inadequate blood supply, severe infection continues with skin discoloration, swelling, pain, and numbness, the symptoms. Debridement, use of antibiotics and hyperbaric oxygen therapy, is the available treatment options. Blood pressure would have dropped. He would have had to be taken to the operating room on probably three occasions to get ahead of the process. Hyperbaric oxygen could have been helpful, but he was never stable enough to tolerate the complexity of the process. His kidney functioning would have deteriorated with rising BUN and low urine output and thoughts of hemodialysis would have been entertained. If…if…if…

(There is such an entity which I used to call my "peripheral brain." For me, it was the Washington Manual on Surgical Diseases which, as a resident, I kept in my white coat pocket. Have you ever seen the surgical textbooks of that era? They weighed three pounds or so. This *manual* was pocket-size with brief summaries of the common surgical diseases and how to manage them. Of course, in 2042, the cell phone was more than just a peripheral brain, and without it, one simply cannot practice or live. Period!)

8

Many new clinicians had been coming and going over the past twenty years of the teaching hospital's clinical staff. Two decades welcomes the new in and gives retirement parties to those departing. Relatively notable and new were Gastroenterologist Joel Harris, fifty-two years old, and a relatively young colorectal surgeon, Fran Robins. Dr. Fran Robins, thirty-eight years old, was a product of the Cleveland Clinic in, for real, Cleveland. (There are satellites of the Mayo Clinic, John's Hopkins, and the Cleveland Clinic in Florida.)

Dr. Mike Mullen, director of the emergency room, was beginning to think he was coming down with something. Just had not been feeling right the past week or longer, Bettie Mullen was concerned. Maybe it is all due to overwork. He never seems able to come home at a decent hour and had not been eating well. She thought that he should see one of the internists. Mike's biggest complaint is abdominal distention. He was uncomfortable wearing a belt around his waist, and he had recently lost a few pounds which he thought was good. He did not tell Bettie that there was some blood on the tissue paper and that he had an OMG moment, remembering medical school days when he had every disease that he studied about. Each year, hundreds of medical students think they have contracted the exact diseases they are studying, but they have not. "Medical students' disease" refers to the phenomenon in which medical students notice something innocuous about their health and then attach to it exaggerated significance. It often corresponds to a disease they have recently learned about in lectures or encountered on the wards.

Bettie made Mike, sixty-three, an appointment to see the gastroenterologist, Dr. Joel Harris, the next week. Mike was encouraged to give himself a good prep cleaning out the colon. Tuesday afternoon, he and Bettie saw Dr. Joel. After he was assured that he had an adequate prep, he had the anesthetist start an IV for "conscious sedation." They turned him on his left side, and the next moment he was wide awake, the colonoscopy was completed. Joel had pictures taken through the endoscope. He had already shown them to Bettie. All Bettie could do was hold Mike's hand...tightly.

When Joel showed Mike the pictures, he freaked out. There was a tumor partially obstructing the lumen of the colon. The gastroenterologist had also taken a few biopsies. The tumor looked to be in the middle of the sigmoid colon. This was high enough that he should not need a colostomy. There was plenty of bowel to work with. So next came the appointment on Friday to see Fran Robins. She was a pleasant, thin, attractive thirty-eight-year-old white female who came right out with it, "When do we operate?" The biopsy was consistent with adenocarcinoma. Since he already had a bowel prep, he was to stay on clear liquids over the next forty-eight hours, and surgery was scheduled for Monday morning. (Her schedule had to be rearranged.) She did not want to have him ruminating over all this, just waiting. Let us get it done, Mike. All agreed.

Lots of calls over the weekend, people praying for him, and relatives he had not heard from in a while. Fran sent him home with a few antianxiety pills and something to help him sleep the night before surgery. (Back in the day, patients were given a sleeper, usually Nembutal at night and another med first thing in the morning, "on call" to the OR. When they were transported to the OR, they were essentially nearly asleep.)

All of Mike's preoperative labs, liver function studies, CXR, and EKG were all good to go. He was asleep in the OR by 7:30 a.m. Monday and awake by 10:30 a.m. All the news was good. There was no gross evidence of spread outside the wall of the bowel, and the liver looked unremarkable. A few shoddy lymph nodes were felt in the mesentery. Pathology should all be done in forty-eight hours, and he was to stay in the hospital for several days on clear liquids. She would see him every day or more if necessary. She told him to work with the inspirometer so as not to get any pulmonary complications. He was up in a chair the following morning, sipping clear liquids and eating Jell-O. He was discharged Saturday morning. A traditional approach gave him a long incision rather than with a laparoscopically-assisted procedure. He was a novice when it came to personal pain, but pain he did have, especially after using the inspirometer. The following Tuesday, he was seen in her office, and they went over the path report which slowed a few enlarged lymph nodes, all negative for cancer. All in all, this was good news. They had gotten it providentially before it had spread, that they were aware of. He would be seen by an oncologist to see if anything further needed to be done. Perhaps just to keep an eye on regular CEA levels, colonic tumor markers.

Dr. Fran was incredibly pleased with how well the surgery had gone. What was next? Something that was missed! It always happens when you try to take extra care of a close friend or relative or colleague or eliminating a step or hurrying time. He should have had a CT scan of the abdomen and pelvis prior to the surgery. Fortunately, or unfortunately, this baseline revealed a two centimeters nodule on the very edge of the right lobe of the liver laterally and posteriorly. It had to be biopsied. It could be a benign growth, but staging is not complete. Dr. Harris felt that the location of the nodule made it probably accessible for laparoscopic removal. It was too soon to operate or even to create a pneumoperitoneum. Surgery was scheduled for two weeks by Dr. Harris and Dr. Robins. Mike was not happy but prayed that it would be manageable; he could not handle much more pain.

Laparoscopically, the right lobe liver nodule was easily resected and proved to be a benign hemangioma. A great sigh of relief. Contemporary practice is to assign stages, a number from 1 to 4 to a cancer, with 1 being an isolated cancer and 4 being a cancer that has spread to the limit of what the assessment measures. The stage generally considers the size of a tumor, whether it has invaded adjacent organs, how many regional (nearby) lymph nodes it has spread to (if any), and whether it has appeared in more distant locations (metastasized). The cancer has not spread to the lymph nodes or nearby tissue. It has reached the outer layers of the colon. But it has not completely grown through.

Adjuvant chemotherapy is not recommended for routine use in patients with stage 2 colon cancer. Follow up in Mike's case: serial CEA levels, colonoscopy within six months, CT scan at six months, yearly CXR. Bettie and Mike were incredibly grateful that the five-year survival rate being close to 90 percent.

It became apparent to Dr. Mike Mullen that he had "dodged a bullet." It also appeared that he would be able to return to work within a relatively short period of time, several weeks. He thought sooner and could be seen in the emergency room in jeans and T-shirt just two weeks after being discharged from the hospital. He was incredibly grateful to his wife for urging him to pursue an answer for his symptoms. (Bettie just happened to be a Proverbs 31 wife.)

Although Fran loved colorectal cancer work, she had a special desire to surgically help those patients with dreaded anal incontinence. These patients are virtually incapacitated; they can go nowhere without having very embarrassing moments. It's best to stay at home. Mostly a disease of aging. I think that is why in the back pew, the last one, there are many worshippers who sit in there for fear of an accident. It's that or watch a program at home by one of your favorite pastors like Charles Stanley and David Jeremiah. Anal incontinence or accidental bowel leakage usually occurs because the anal sphincter and pelvic floor muscles are not functioning properly. The anal sphincter muscle is a circular muscle that surrounds the anal canal, and the pelvic floor muscles (levator ani) form a sling around the anal canal. Both the anal sphincter and pelvic floor muscles help women control their stools. Damage to these muscles is usually attributed to childbirth and/or aging. The muscles may be torn or the nerves that help them function may well be damaged leading to impaired function of the continence mechanism.

Sometimes, anal sphincter injuries are recognized in the delivery room; however, often they are not as obvious and do not become a problem until later in life. Many women may experience anal incontinence from loss of muscle strength as they get older. An anal sphincteroplasty repairs the tear in the sphincter muscle and rebuilds the perineal body (area between the rectum and vagina). It does not require any incisions on the abdomen, and women go home from the hospital on the same day as surgery. There are so many people with anal incontinence who do not know it's fixable if they will see someone like Dr. Fran. She literally could have a clinic one or two days a month just for evaluation as to what is available to control these very embarrassing fears. How many bright, sharp, intelligent elderly folks could be contributing to society were it not for this problem. Many become a recluse, "not giving up meeting together, as some are in the habit of doing, but encouraging one another-and all the more as you see the Day approaching" (Hebrews 10:25).

Dr. Suzanne Grayson would often have patients with the relaxed pelvic floor. She was glad the good doctor was around. Dr. Grayson scrubbed in on a few of Fran's cases. Dr. Grayson and her partner Veronica Lacy still worked a bit at University Hospital but spend much of their time at the teaching hospital in New Fledgling, doing surgery, and as attendings, they had a great part in the education of the medical students as well as residents and interns. They were a great asset as attendings. Always like a hen with her chicks. These two were just about the only gynecologists in the New Fledgling area.

Sally, the boys' mother was dying, and during that period, Storz had gone ahead and had the boys baptized into the Jehovah's Witness faith. Jesus told his followers to "make disciples of people of all the nations" (Matthew 28:19, 20). When he sent out his early disciples, Jesus directed them to go to the homes of the people (Matthew 10:7, 11–13). After Jesus's death, first-century Christians continued to spread their message both "publicly and from house to house" (Acts 5:42, 20:20). Those of the *faith* follow the example of those early Christians and find that the door-to-door ministry is a good way to reach people.

Jehovah's Witnesses have their own Bible, the New World Translation. Just with one verse and you can understand their main belief. There are several verses with a completely different meaning than other translations, such as John 1:1.

> In [the] beginning the Word was, and the Word was with God, and the Word was *a* god. (JW)

Quite different than the NIV translation: "In the beginning was the Word, and the Word was with God, and the Word was God" (NIV). Jehovah's Witnesses do not believe in the Trinity as we know it. For them, Jesus is the "first created being of God." He is not equal to God but is *a* god. God's holy spirit operates only as he directs it (Luke 11:13). The Bible also compares God's spirit to water and associates it with such things as faith and knowledge. These comparisons all point to the impersonal nature of the Holy Spirit. The Holy Spirit is not a person they believe (Isaiah 44:3; Acts 6:5; 2 Corinthians 6:6).

9

There was no next of kin immediately known for Sergeant Poley. No one had accompanied him to the hospital. He had no visitors. He had never been married. There was no way to contact anyone. After the demise, the question finally arose as to next of kin. The VH had nothing in the record about any family. The VH was doing due service in trying to find kin even though a suit was in the back of everyone's mind. But the forty-two-year-old army sergeant must have records from the service, and great effort was made to find someone to claim the deceased. The morgue needed direction. The sergeant's soul was not settled. No closure with death. No funeral or memorial service.

And then, a sister's name was found on one document, his enlistment record. A Matty Stebbins in Lexington, Kentucky. This Matty Stebbins was unfortunately more than just a phone call away. Several hours passed before contact was eventually made. When contacted, circumstances were strange as Matty was being summoned to the phone. It happened to be a neighbor's phone number in the next room which Matty always used for any important calls (which never happened). When contact was finally made, Ms. Stebbins seemed unemotional regarding news of the death of her estranged brother. She asked for the circumstances and parties involved, recommended that a military burial be accomplished for her *dear* brother whom she had not heard from in fifteen years or longer. She requested contact persons information, specifically asking for phone numbers for the administration of the VH.

The events surrounding Poley's death were impossible to convey to Ms. Stebbins over the phone, and it was recommended that she come to the hospital. She was suspicious because of the vagueness of what she was hearing, not understanding. Yes, she has a psychiatric history. But she was not at all stupid. She thought for a few moments. She then said to hold off the burial of her brother until she came to town. The VH offered to pay the expenses for her transportation which further increased her suspicion. As she was obviously not pleased, "getting the run-a-round," she would somehow make plans for the trip two states away. She *lived* in a domicile, and she referred to herself as Ms. Matty. At irregular hours of the day or evening, she could be seen pushing a shopping cart (confiscated from a grocery store chain) with an array of contents (her treasures) found along her *route* back to the domicile. She had a room at the *home* paid for by the government. She owned the dress she was wearing, and she and the clothes both needed a bath. How in the world could she possibly manage to get to the VH?

As she walked away from the neighbor's phone in the domicile, mulling over things, she was summoned back to the phone for another caller. This caller introduced herself as Ms. Judy Newhouse, an attorney calling from the Veterans Hospital's office of the chief of staff. Ms. Newhouse of Prudential Life Insurance Company was notifying Ms. Stebbins of a $100,000 life insurance policy taken out by her deceased brother, listing Matty as the beneficiary. Ms. Newhouse had been informed by the VH administration of what Matty's circumstances might be, living in a domicile in another state. Suspecting the worst-case scenario, Ms. Newhouse suggested that they should meet and that she was willing to come to see her and perhaps assist her in the best course of action on behalf of Matty's deceased loved one. Ms. Newhouse did not want to leave Matty in the lurch, so she got address information and told her not to take any more calls, and she would come as soon as she could get a flight out, probably in a day or two.

You must realize that decades ago people referring to themselves or were being referred to as *bag ladies* or, in the case of men, a *bum* would be not homeless but hospitalized in the many "insane asylums" in the country. They flourished but perhaps that phrase also applies to another class of institutions meant to house those deemed unfit for society—mental asylums. And for centuries—right up until the present day in some places—the quality of most mental asylums, at least those in the European tradition, revealed little degree of civilization at all. When they all closed, around 1955, these people had no place to turn without help, so they still lived in the woods, making them difficult to count. Why did the asylums close?

Over the near century, *deinstitutionalization* has helped create the mental illness crisis by discharging people from public psychiatric hospitals without ensuring that they received the medication and rehabilitation services necessary for them to live successfully in the community. Deinstitutionalization further exacerbated the situation because once the public psychiatric beds had been closed, they were not available for people who later became mentally ill, and this situation continues up to the present. And consequently, approximately 2.2 million severely mentally ill people do not receive any psychiatric treatment. These people used to be arrested for some vague crime because you knew at least they would be put in a facility where they would get food and shelter. You don't invent a crime, but it is a discretionary decision. You might not arrest everybody for it, but you know that way they will be safe and fed. Of course, taking care of all homeless persons will always be a problem: "For you always have the poor with you, and whenever you want, you can do good to them; but you do not always have Me" (Mark 14:7 NASB).

An (anonymous) member of the Los Angeles police force described frequent arrests of severely mentally ill homeless persons:

> They are suffering from malnutrition, with dirt-encrusted skin and hair or bleeding from open wounds. It is really pitiful. You get people who are hallucinating, who have not eaten for days. It is a massive cleanup effort. They get shelter, food, and you get them back on their medications. It is crisis intervention. Welcome to the current homeless situation without solution even now in 2042, but more than ever is the problem. Closure of the asylums left no place for the per-

> sons to live and no way to get appropriate medications. We created this. They are homeless and hopeless, and truthfully, some prefer to live that way, supported in some fashion by the government (you and me!).

Several very anxious hours and a few days passed before Ms. Matty Stebbins arrived at the Veterans Hospital. She had met Judy Newhouse, and they had traveled to a nearby mall where two new dresses and a few other necessary items were bought and paid for by Ms. Newhouse. (Quite a few items including a tote bag.) She bought each a one-way ticket headed east.

A conference was setup involving Ms. Newhouse (as Matty's attorney) and Col. Todd Fraser, MD JAG officer, representing the VH.

The Uniform Code of Military Justice is the governing document for legal matters in the military and is a bit different than the civilian code. JAG officers serve as military lawyers, but only the most highly educated, intelligent, and dedicated individuals make the cut.

Officers in the Army Judge Advocate General's Corps (JAGC) are practicing attorneys who handle military legal matters. JAG Corps attorneys enter the army as officers after graduation from law school, and the army trains them in military law and procedures.

Attorney Sandra Standstill, MD, JD of Phallon and Associates, would be representing Dr. Freidman and the Teaching Hospital of San Petra (Friedman's employer). Dr. Friedman's name was prominent though he had not laid eyes on the sergeant, his name was part of the record as he was an employee of the teaching hospital as chief of infectious diseases. Ms. Stebbins, in her late fifties chronologically but not well cared for, did not attend the conference. She would have nothing which would be pertinent to the case, so she was kept busy touring the facility and having lunch.

Obviously, Ms. Newhouse was more than just a representative of a life insurance company. The one hundred thousand dollars rightfully would belong to Ms. Stebbins, and those details would be worked out in time. No, this was a seemingly strong medical malpractice case involving multiple persons and what was needed was a strong medical malpractice mind. Also present, Sandra Standstill, an experienced trial attorney with an MD as well as JD, would add much to the case. She would diligently research the situation and the disease process that took the life of the sergeant. Both Standstill and Newhouse are teamed up supporting Matty (representing her deceased brother laying in a drawer in the VH morgue, awaiting orders), Dr. Friedman and the teaching hospital against the mighty medical/military knowhow of the defense. Col. Todd Frazer defending the Veterans Hospital, Chief Resident Rogers, Dr. Smith, and the third-year medical student, Erin.

Speaking for the young intern Dr. Smith and Chief Resident Rogers and the VH, Colonel Todd realized that Fournier's was an extremely rare and confusing entity. What is the mortality rate for this disease? Could have or should have the case been handled differently to result in a better prognosis for the life of Sergeant Poley?

10

Gerald Fleeger had been waiting for some communication with the next of kin and the attorneys for Sergeant Poley. Dr. Fleeger is a sixty-seven-year-old Caucasian man who has been a pathologist almost his whole life. After retiring from the military, he took this job. He remembers "back in the day" when autopsies were in, especially at the VH. Every death went to the morgue and had the postmortem exam including the *skullcap* exposing the brain.

Before the technology such as the CAT scan, often clinicians were not certain as to the diagnosis of diseases. For instance, the saying "pus somewhere, pus nowhere, pus beneath the diaphragm." Diagnosis was not always forthcoming, and family wanted an answer. They also made it almost comedic like opening the stomach to see what the patient had for supper. (I remember the pungent aroma of gastric juice, blood, alcohol, and stool.) A new class of medical students and nursing students jumped at the opportunity to see this pathologist in action along with his ever-present Diener, Washington Jones. Washington, having been there twenty-five illustrious years, was nearing his final days. He had smoked like almost everybody to some degree. Lung cancer took many of the Hollywood black-and-white movie stars like Humphry Bogart and Yul Brynner. John Wayne along with Yul and Humphrey made pleas on black-and-white TVs, urging adoring fans to quit and do not ever start, to please stop smoking. Others, celebrity smokers of cigarettes especially the non-filtered cigarettes who died of lung cancer: Suzanne Pleshette, Anne Francis, Susan Hayward, Martha Hyer, Vincent Price, Desi Arnaz, Nat King Cole, Chuck Connors.

Ms. Matty Stebbins wanted to identify the brother she had not laid eyes on for nearly two decades, and there were two teams of attorneys wanting to get to the point and get this over with. Sergeant Poley lay frozen in drawer 3 in the morgue at the Veterans Hospital. He did not have a schedule. It was Ms. Newhouse who would escort Ms. Stebbins to the morgue in the dank, dark, cold, and eerie basement.

And that was how the long-awaited reunion would go. After introductions, drawer 3 was slid open. The plastic drape covering Sergeant Poley's frozen body was pulled back revealing the face down to the shoulders.

"That is not my brother!" exclaimed Ms. Stebbins. "I remember when Patrick joined the army, he got his first tattoo, a cross and serpent on one of his forearms. He was so proud of it."

With a nod from the pathologist, the morgue Diener pulled the cloudy, rubbery, somewhat thick greasy drape down to expose the deceased one's stiff arms. Stiff as he was, he had to be turned to expose the backs of his arms, and it also would expose the area of the body that took his life. Tough old woman as Ms. Stebbins was, she fainted and hit the floor with a thud. After she regained herself, she insisted that the body was not that of her long-lost brother. There were no tattoos on the body of Sergeant Poley. She hit her head on the concrete floor of the morgue the second time she looked at the body...another louder thud this time which lacerated her skull and couldn't be aroused because she was pulseless.

Or was she?

Well, for a moment or three, Matty did appear to have sustained a sizeable laceration, and she was motionless, barely breathing. Blood was flowing all over the morgue Diener as he tried to lift her off the floor, and onto a cold hard *stretcher*, she looked dead. A code blue was called from the morgue in the dank, dark, etc.... I think you get the picture. A code in the morgue must top all the events over the years. She stirred a bit. (No, the Diener was not a faith healer.) Why in the world would there be a need for a code cart in the morgue, and where was it kept? Who was the bright one that envisioned this need and kept it updated just like the sign in the Otis Elevator in plain view with initials signifying it was up to date?

Well, soon commotion, footsteps running with the code cart over the dirty, worn concrete floor. *Matty is alive?* She was breathing, and when attached to the monitor, she did have an awfully slow bradycardia but no open airway. They lifted her chin to open her airway. Now that she could have her breath more easily, it allowed her to speak, "Get me the hell out of here." And off they went as she seemed to lose consciousness a bit more hurried to the emergency room but not before the pathologist informed whomever the facts that "I'm not certain, but I do believe and will dictate for the record that Ms. Stebbins had positively identified her brother from the faded tattoo on the skin barely visible on the left forearm, appearing to be, yes, a cross and a serpent!"

It wasn't long before Judy Newhouse got a handle on her frightened self, and she was composed enough to be guided to the VH administration office. The code team's slow speed suggested that Ms. Matty was stabilizing. The emergency room staff hurried through the ABCs which by now were quite normal. She had a ten centimeter long laceration behind the left ear to the occipital area to the bone of the skull. Pressure applied until the doctor felt no skull fracture. The laceration was repaired with a somnolent Ms. Matty and lots of local anesthesia.

Where does Ms. Matty travel from here? The chief of staff was becoming more confused as the situation seemed to change minute to minute. But things were in progress. First, Matty was sent, after the emergency room visit, to the postanesthesia recovery room for monitoring purpose and a small amount of sedation as she was getting a bit rambunctious, her wrists were restrained, and she was appropriately sedated. There came a call from the x-ray department that they were ready to do a brain CT scan, and she made her next step into the CT machine. The radiologist was waiting to view the images as they came on the computer screen. It was a positive scan! There was no cerebral bleeding, but Matty had a small subdural hematoma.

If that were the diagnosis, next scene was a pretty lady with head swathed in white bandage. It brought back memories of Dr. Ben Casey who, every Friday night on our TV screen, would have an attractive patient over which Ben and Dr. Zorba would have a discussion as to what to do with this patient. This was back in the late fifties; no one were yet conceived of an x-ray with computer images. Well, frankly there were no computers yet, only the giant ones at the jet propulsion lab. A film of the skull might show a fracture, but more than likely, Ben Casey would determine the lovely patient to have either bad news, or she was just another lovely lady who was simply hysterical for those were the only two diagnoses in the scripts as yet.

These were fascinating, challenging, years for all fields of medicine and surgery because of a couple of things. First, in the awake patient able to describe the illness was the SOAP note.

S—Subjectively, the diagnosis could be made simply on the basis of what the patient told you by 80–85 percent.

O—Objectively. Then your physical exam up to maybe 90 percent.

Then some basic lab tests like a complete blood count (CBC), primarily looking for the abnormal white count signifying infection and the low hemoglobin suggesting bleeding or anemia. Physical diagnosis was the main stay of clinical medicine. For the neurologist, percussion hammers, tuning forks, and a sharp needle for sensory checks. The pupils especially important and, of course, the skin color or presence of a rash. (As medical students back in the seventies, we were given the black doctor's bag, percussion hammer, tuning fork, and a sharp needle. I don't remember carrying the bag. I have baseball cards in my black bag…ancient.)

Chest x-ray to diagnose pneumonia, and believe this or not, an x-ray of the skull to visualize the rare calcified pineal gland checking for a midline shift of the brain. This was a real zebra almost never found. The pineal gland sets itself apart from other intracranial structures due to accumulation of levels of calcium and fluoride in the circulation. A positive shift of that centrally located intracranial mass was a rare thing of beauty for the diagnostician.

A—It is your assessment that is your tentative diagnosis.

P—It is your plan. How will you (tentatively) treat the patient?

There, in a nutshell, was the SOAP note from your H & P.

Today it's all a phone call to the neurologist, that the CT of the brain is normal or abnormal, before he/she will evaluate the patient.

How are things in the clinical environment of health issues as we are into 2042?

Well, there are no diagnosticians. None needed! You don't have to decide what Michelangelo was blatantly trying to say from the synapse between God's welcoming, directing finger and the hesitant, lazy finger of humankind. That space is either half full or half empty. If only man could straighten out his finger to touch God's, I think that we all would go to heaven. He said that he would, and that all would come to repentance. But the man who gave us King David and the Sistine Chapel essence of life calls us to fill that space with as much love and peace that the Lord had/has for the believer.

Now the phone that we carry in our hand the day through has taken the place of diagnostician and patient alike. We don't need to ever touch a patient or see him up close, the phone is "on call" 24–7 nonstop. Robotics thirty years ago. Artificial intelligence is young, but the possibilities of our own flawed mind will be replaced by errorless machinery. Patient care will never be the same.

Back to the present case of Ms. Matty Stebbins. She is sedated and restrained and has a small subdural hematoma? A board question on the orals.

How about a continuous *streaming* CT scan or MRI to visualize what that subdural hematoma does moment by moment. Of course, we could just have two of the students rotating through the neurology service to keep checking for soft changes in her clinical status. "What does the scan tell us about Matty from moment to moment? Q ten-minute CT images times twenty-four hours. There are such things as chronic subdural hematomas. Let's say that neurologically she remains stable in no need of surgical intervention.

Right now, we just need to evaluate Matty to determine her future. There is, of course, the matter of the $100,000 life insurance policy. I can't imagine how high the settlement could be as the suit progresses.

11

Can the government be sued over questionable medical malpractice? Joining the military comes with a certain understanding of risk to life and limb. But did you know that service members, or their families on their behalf, can't always sue the military if they are injured, permanently disabled, or killed because of negligence *off* the battlefield? Pat Poley was an army sergeant injured off the battlefield when he died of a "flesh-eating bacterial infection" known as Fournier's gangrene.

While the deceased's sister got ready for the trip, she had contacted a local law firm for advice. It was recommended because of her suspicion that she should consider hiring a civilian law firm with military experience before considering filing a claim against the government. She heard the term *Feres Doctrine* for the first time. It is a case of accountability. With the passage of the National Defense Authorization Act of 2019, military servicemen and women could now file claims against the government for medical malpractice committed by military doctors.

This law effectively overrules the Feres Doctrine, which previously barred legal action against the government for military medical malpractice. Congress partially overturned the doctrine, prohibiting troops from filing negligence lawsuits against the military in December of 2019 when it voted on a defense authorization bill that allows victims to file claims in cases of medical malpractice but not in other circumstances. A Green Beret from Fort Bragg, North Carolina, has been fighting for his life and led the effort to eliminate the Feres Doctrine and allow active duty and retired military to sue the government for military medical malpractice.

(On April 30, 2019, the sergeant first class, Richard Stayskal, testified before the House Armed Services Committee in Washington, DC, at a hearing called, "Feres Doctrine. A Policy in Need of Reform?"

Stayskal's story is a heartbreaking tragedy.

Stayskal is a Purple Heart recipient with stage 4 lung cancer. His cancer was missed in a January 2017 physical at Army Medical Center. It was said that doctors failed to identify a large tumor in the upper-right lobe of his lung during a CT scan.

Shortly after the physical, Stayskal's health declined, and six months later, he was diagnosed with terminal cancer.

In the hearing, Stayskal told the committee, "The failure of the military doctor's gross negligence and failure to detect and treat my cancer when it was first noted on the CT done on me in January 2017 is the mistake that allowed the aggressive tumor to double in size and rob me and my family of my life without any recourse due to a 1950 Supreme Court case that created the Feres Doctrine." Stayskal has a wife and two daughters.

During the hearing, he also said, "I want to say that this does affect me obviously, but my children are the true victims." Stayskal's daughters are getting special treatment and counseling at school while trying to understand how this could have happened to their father. (https://justicecounts.com/personal-injury/what-is-the-feres-doctrine-for-military-medical-malpractice).

Obviously, this had direct bearing involving that week's horror adding further to the seriousness of this mystery. Admit it or not, urgency was needed in solving this series almost tantamount to possible manslaughter cases. What did the death of the good sergeant have to do with this? Was his case the source of all of this? The five infected patients' caste a grim shadow over the entire hospital and spread to the teaching hospital forty so miles away as well. Could this conceivably ever happen again? The sergeant's drainage causing the Fournier's gangrene perhaps were linked but certainly not on purpose. Time was of the essence to avoid any further damage, death, and embarrassment.

Institutional problems of this nature are often swept under the rug and had been for years of the Veterans Hospitals. The policy invoked with demanding that all complications and deaths were to be investigated since 2019. With the implementation of the National Defense Authorization Act of 2019, military servicemen and women could now file claims against the government for medical malpractice committed by military doctors. This was a long time coming. The John S. McCain National Defense Authorization Act for Fiscal Year 2019 (NDAA 2019) is a United States federal law which specifies the budget, expenditures, and policies of the US Department of Defense (DOD) for fiscal year 2019. It was signed by Donald Trump during a ceremony in Fort Drum, New York, on August 13, 2018.

The conference room was abuzz and crowded compared with recent M & M Conferences. The sergeant received top billing, and after the discussion of Fournier's and comments from the physicians and students, the VA contingent departed to take care of their current patients' treatments and further evaluation. How was this puzzle, this deadly *exercise* to be looked at again? The *vector*, an organism, typically a biting insect or tick, transmits a disease or parasite from one animal or plant to another. In this case, the transmission was human with an agenda and using bacteria to accomplish his/her purpose. What could possibly be the motive to do such a horrible thing and how did they do it?

What exactly has gone on that is factual? At the time of the first procedure, there did not appear to be a specimen except for a lap full of pus when the perirectal abscess was *drained* (inadequately) by the third-year medical student. The intern on this case was urgently called away to the emergency room, so he did not exactly see what the student had done. The intern did the proper incision and drainage procedure that Tuesday when the terribly ill sergeant was returned to surgery. The specimen was handled correctly this time and cultures of the pus grew all three of the suspect organisms.

Teaching hospitals offer some of the best care in the country. They are committed to excellent patient care, as well as teaching medical students to become excellent future physicians. All teaching hospitals deal with high turnover rates, especially as students rotate between medical specialties or leave the training program. This change rate in staffing can make it difficult for even the best hospitals and physicians to professionally train and/or monitor students and interns. When students have various training and expertise levels but limited monitoring, errors are likely to occur.

Although medical students can be sued by a medical malpractice attorney for medical errors, they are unlikely to be held liable since they are not licensed medical professionals. It is not surprising then that there are more mistakes in any hospital training future docs happening at the start of July when turnover occurs. Not a perfect time to schedule your surgery!

(The beeper went off Sunday night around ten. It seemed like an opportune time to move again. Things had quieted somewhat, but now the investigation was ramping up [lawyers]. The camera's disabled and the remainder of the solution mixed, the long steel table was wheeled back to CS. The select rooms cases instrument packs (1, 3, 5, 7, 9) were unwrapped and the same procedure spraying the solution on the instruments on the rolled towel. The actual initial purulent specimen had been kept as pure as possible on agar plates kept in the step-down lab. The solution should have retained the initial virulence. There was a sixth instrument pack labeled "Emergency Laparotomy" on the table. This too was treated. This instrument pack was kept in a special area. It was wrapped in red cloth material. It was left on the steel table. After removing all traces of this intrusion, the steel table placed back in position, and the toggle switch was placed on enabling the camera's system.)

12

Tragedy happened at the Veterans Hospital again, but this time it was suspected as early as Wednesday and Friday. The rooms were the odd numbered ones in the surgical suite on Monday morning's schedule.

Partial Operating Room Schedule for Monday (six weeks from first horror)

Room 1. 58 YO M left total knee (increased pain, fever to 103, Wednesday)

Room 3. 46 YO M arthroscopic RT shoulder repair rotator cuff (pain, fever 102, Wednesday)

Room 5. 40 YO M RT hemicolectomy S/P appy with carcinoid (pain, fever 102.5, Thursday)

Room 7. 70 YO F anal sphincteroplasty, Dr. Fran on Vet (deceased found at home, Wednesday)

Room 9. 80 YO M open gastrostomy (cellulitis, pain, fever 101, Friday)

This was too complicated to present at any conference by Saturday's M & M. None of these patients were transferred to any other facility as none were desperately ill. But you could bet the VH was in the process of looking at each case, trying to first get a handle on the cases for the proper treatment of all these complicated, infected patients coming from odd numbered OR rooms from Monday.

Mildred was a frail seventy-year-old female who had retired from the Nursing Corps as a captain several years ago and had requested both Dr. Fran Robins and Dr. Grayson to be her surgeons.

She requested that she be "knocked out" for the procedure. She was given conscious sedation appropriately. A few absorbable sutures were used for the sphincteroplasty, and she quickly awakened. Marcaine, a longer acting local anesthetic agent, was used at the operative site for early post-op discomfort. She was discharged later that day to be seen by Dr. Fran on Thursday morning in her office at the teaching hospital in New Fledgling.

That Tuesday after surgery, she was in a great deal of pain. That was unexpected and the Extra Strength Tylenol did not help. She phoned Dr. Fran's service. Someone covering for her ordered a stronger medication which the patient's daughter picked up from an all-night pharmacy. Turns out the patient later that night took one pill which did not help her pain. She then took two more pills five minutes apart which unfortunately were opioid medications. Patient has a history of chronic obstructive pulmonary disease and has a pacemaker for history of cardiac arrhythmia. After that third dose of pain pills, her pain finally disappeared while this thin, fragile smoker developed bradycardia, became somnolent, quit breathing, and quietly passed away. The daughter called her early Wednesday morning, and with no answer, she thought her mom, who was also hearing impaired due to age, just was not wide awake yet. When no answer to calls through the day, a granddaughter was sent to only find grandmother cold, stiff, and dead. Dr. Fran's office was called, shocking Dr. Fran. She was terribly alarmed, expecting this case to be very benign. Not so.

Paula had excitedly phoned the chief of staff to be seen that Thursday after hearing about the deceased patient and the news of the incident happening the second time. She had an urgent request to bring to the chief's attention. Thursday afternoon, she was extremely nervous and upset. Attached with sterilization tape to the window of the Central Supply entrance door was a cryptic note created out of magazine pages, letters cut out to create a disturbing message that simply read:

PAULA U SHOULD'VE
SEEN THIS COMING

The same modus operandi: all different rooms; different surgeons, nurses, and surgical technicians; different procedures; and different time from surgery to symptoms and signs of infection. Cultures of incisional wounds would grow the same bacteria as that which was cultured from the initial case of the sergeant's incision and drainage of the perirectal horseshoe abscess nearly six weeks ago. How could this possibly have happened again, now with probably a related death although final diagnosis would be pending autopsy? Murder at the Veterans Hospital?

The Veterans Hospital surgical suite was closed until further notice.

13

This unfortunate patient was a seventy-year-old white female with chronic fecal and urinary incontinence who had complained of worsening symptoms mainly due to both lack of flatus control and fecal incontinence essentially causing her to become a recluse. She was helped by an indwelling urinary catheter. Her chronic cough kept her prisoner in her own home. Still smoking! She had comorbid diagnoses of chronic obstructive pulmonary disease (low-flow oxygen supplement dependent) and cardiac arrhythmias with a demand pacemaker. Dr. Fran Robins had reviewed the literature prior to scheduling Mildred A. for a sphincteroplasty. Sphincteroplasty, in the treatment of patients with fecal incontinence due to anal sphincter defects, has been questioned because the success rate declines in the long-term. There had been some early success with sacral nerve stimulation. The data available so far on the long-term success rate after sacral nerve modulation do not differ substantially from those after sphincteroplasty. Mildred also had an issue with urinary control and, for some time, has been depended on an indwelling Foley catheter.

Reading through several articles comparing the two procedures, Fran felt the data did not support the replacement of sphincteroplasty with sacral nerve stimulation in patients with fecal incontinence secondary to sphincter defects.

Dr. Robins was concerned the patient was becoming more despondent over her "problem," that the coughing, which really magnifies the anal symptoms conceivably, would increase the likelihood of failure with this surgical procedure. Mildred and her family, thinking rightfully so that this was going to be a benign process, decided that it was worth trying. Mildred haply was looking forward to the surgery. She missed going to church even though she sat in the last pew; the ambience was telling and embarrassing. She was miserable.

But what really happened to cause Mildred's death? This factor alone made it critical to investigate the short post-op course. At first gut feeling, Fran could not concede that the anesthesia or the operation was the cause of the patient's demise. Fran held a meeting with the family the day after her death to find out what they knew during those hours when the patient complained of worsening pain at the surgical site. Her pain may have been out of proportion to what was to be expected by late the night of the procedure. The Marcaine, a long-acting local anesthetic, had worn off by late evening, and she had only been instructed to take extra strength Tylenol for her post-op pain. Although we can only surmise the events of those twenty-four to thirty-six hours, it was highly likely that her normal coughing would have led to increased pain, and although the family would not agree to an autopsy, it was possible the repaired sphincter muscular sutures likely failed.

Unfortunately, all that said, the real cause of death, which without an autopsy is impossible to absolutely prove, most likely would be due to opioid overdosing.

As Mildred had been dependent on an indwelling urinary catheter, a sample obtained through fresh urine would possibly be helpful. How long can opioids be detected in urine? Urine testing shows this drug being detectable one to three days for opioids, depending on the specific drug. Certain opioids may be detectable for less than one day after use, and some opioids will be detected for longer than three days after last use. This time frame will depend on the specific test cutoff and particular opioid used as well.

And just a wild guess, this would be arguable if ever brought to trial from the standpoint of the Veterans Hospital. However, the real culprit was the opioid medication and what could happen to the doctor, covering for Dr. Fran, who ordered the medication over the phone. We found out that the surgeon covering only ordered one tablet to be given at a time, eight hours apart, and the patient was responsible for her own demise…since she did not follow "orders."

We would never know. Did the prescribing physician err in ordering that medication? Arguable! They did not know the patient, which brought up that subject of coverage. A frail seventy-year-old lady with COPD, still smoking with a pacemaker, died from an opioid overdose. This early in her post-op course, she should at least have had a visiting nurse to observe and to oversee her medications. We didn't know the ramifications of the case because there was no one assisting in her care. Perhaps the family should have thought something was going on when she hadn't answered the phone.

Time wise, it is important to note that this case had nothing to do with the horrors of what had happened the past weeks in the operating rooms. Odds are probable that had she lived, she would have had to deal with, for her, the same fate as the others operated on that Monday. In the multiple cases over that period, this was the first death. You can say that the VH is off the hook on this seriously ramp-up scenario, but the fact remains that she was a post-op patient, and the hospital was where she was when she had her surgery. The Veterans Hospital is responsible, unless a perpetrator for all the operative patients' infections is found, how can there be any trial in the future? Dr. Fran had learned a great lesson that Saturday morning, for she would see plenty of these cases in the future, hopefully with a better outcome and certainly, not a fatality. Literature on sacral nerve stimulation may be a valid approach in fecal incontinence due to sphincter lesions when compared to sphincteroplasty repair. The next fecal incontinence septuagenarian patient presenting to Dr. Fran will be treated differently. I'd be willing to bet!

Mildred's unfortunate case was to be presented at the next morbidity and mortality conference on Saturday morning at the teaching hospital in New Fledgling. Morbidity and mortality conferences have long been part of the practice of medicine, having originated in the early 1900s with Ernest Codman at Massachusetts General Hospital in Boston. He was questioned, "What nerve he had to suggest evaluating the competence of surgeons?" As a result, Dr. Codman lost his staff privileges! You must know that surgeons didn't even wear sterile gloves or any gloves until thanks to the work of Halsted at the end of the nineteenth century (in spite of his narcotic addiction). In 1889, one nurse at the Johns Hopkins Hospital in Baltimore found that constant washing of her hands and surgical instruments in carbolic acid was giving her dermatitis. To save her from having to continually expose her hands to the acid, the surgeon in chief, William Stewart Halsted, designed and commissioned a rubber glove from the Goodyear Rubber Company.

Ignaz Semmelweis, in the midnineteenth century, solved childbed fever by having doctors wash their hands between autopsy and examination of otherwise healthy pregnant women at delivery. He was scorned, his sincere work was laughed at, and he was determined by his peers that he must be insane. He was placed in a Viennese insane asylum and died from injuries sustained from multiple beatings.

Several issues with reference to Mildred's care were covered in depth: a frail seventy-year-old woman should not have had the surgery with so much comorbidity; electrical stimulation of those perianal muscles should have been used rather than a surgical procedure, knowing that she would be coughing which would probably disrupt the repair; if there was to be surgical repair, the patient should have been kept in the hospital postoperatively where her pain would be better controlled at least overnight with milder medications and lidocaine ointment at the operative site. Perhaps mild sedation might have helped with the coughing. She would more carefully have been evaluated for pain relief and treated more appropriately. The on-call surgeon should never have used opioids in such a frail patient with heart and lung disease. He should have sent her back to the hospital where she could have had more appropriate evaluation and treatment.

A minor procedure? There are no minor procedures. The retrospectoscope is always twenty-twenty. Bottom line, never consider any thing you do as a surgeon to be minor especially in the very elderly and the very young. Usually there are half a dozen cases to be presented. This patient and her care gave everyone pause to consider the whole situation regarding patient care. The conference was adjourned early. Take nothing for granted in the practice of medicine and surgery.

14

The Teaching Hospital of New Fledgling, now in its second decade, has not only attracted the brightest minds but stands in the forefront of research as well. Particularly, that of noninvasive heart valve replacement as well as thoracic and abdominal aortic aneurysm repair. The vascular surgery as well as the cardiovascular department have attracted the best. Here in the fourth decade of the twenty-first century, there is active research still trying for the least invasive but always aware of the pitfalls and attempt to keep the program one of the lowest morbidity and mortality. Nothing ventured, nothing gained. For instance, open repair of the ruptured aneurysm carries with an unacceptable mortality. It has been shown that EVAR has a better prognosis for the free ruptured aneurysm. Opening the abdomen releases the tamponade the patient's blood pressure will plumate and hence a high mortality. With endovascular repair with a tamponade abdomen, chances are for decreasing the mortality, that is, if the patient can get to the proper medical facility. It's a moot point at that stage. The endovascular aneurysm repair done by the trained vascular surgeon with the elective repair of nonruptured aneurysms carries with it a better result but still with a 30 percent complication rate. There is always the possibility of occlusive bilateral renal blood flow should the endovascular prosthesis migrate cephalad compromising those vessels with the result of renal failure and hemodialysis. Always the worst-case scenario would be death!

Dr. George Michaels knocked on the door to exam room 3 of the surgical clinic at the Teaching Hospital in New Fledgling. He was there on a vascular consult from Dr. Rex Swiss for a sixty-one-year-old man with an enlarging, possibly symptomatic abdominal aortic aneurysm. He had presented to his internist with symptoms consistent with gallstone disease and a dynamic sonogram of the abdomen had revealed a six centimeters AAA. Previously within six months ago, the aneurysm was noted on sonogram but now appeared to be just one centimeter larger. He had no back pain, only upper right quadrant tenderness associated with acute cholecystitis.

Dr. Michaels entered the room to find a moderately obese sixty-one-year-old Caucasian male in no distress but certainly a bit nervous. "I'm Dr. Michaels, Jason 'Marks.' Do you know why you are here?"

Jason was uncertain, a bit confused at this point. After looking at Jason's wristband, he shook Jason's sweaty palm. George wanted not to alarm the patient, but the diagnosis was of some concern.

"Jason, tell me a little about your history," Dr. Michaels asked.

Jason replied that he was the owner of a construction company and continually active in the job. He related that he had two stents, the result of a heart attack two years ago, that he took one baby aspirin each morning and that he was not particularly good at keeping up with his fingerstick glucose levels.

"So you have type two diabetes, and you are a smoker?"

Embarrassed, Jason relates smoking two packs of cigarettes for forty years and that he had tried to quit many times.

Dr. Michaels replied, "We can take care of that for you after we take care of why you are here."

The doctor asked what kind of symptoms had brought Jason to the clinic that day.

Jason replied, "Well, Doc, it's weird. Sometimes I have this very full feeling in my belly, and I swear that I can feel my heartbeat if I put my hands on my belly. Sometimes, it keeps me awake at night. There are a couple of ulcers on my feet that do not seem to fully heal. They don't hurt particularly. It might look painful but really not so. Okay, Doc, so what do we need to do?"

"Well, there are two ways we can take care of your aneurysm. One involves putting you to sleep, then I make a large incision." Dr. Michaels pointed to Jason's lower sternum all the way down to his navel. "Then I will place a clamp above and below the aneurysm, cut open the aneurysm, and sew a long tube graft inside. The graft will start just below your kidney arteries and travel down to where your leg arteries branch off your aorta. Then I will sew your diseased aorta back around the graft, remove the clamps check for any leaks, and we're good to go. You'll be in the hospital for a week to ten days."

Jason blurted out, "A week or so? I can't miss that much work!"

"Jason, this is profoundly serious! You could die! The risk of you dying from the surgery is about 8 percent."

"Okay, what's the other option?"

Dr. Michaels finally sat down in the chair and pulled it closer to Jason. "Okay, so the other approach is called EVAR or endovascular aneurysm repair. We do those in the hybrid OR suite. In this room, we can do open surgeries, and we have access to an x-ray or fluoroscopy machine. For EVAR, you are awake but relaxed. I will make a small incision in each groin."

Dr. Michaels pointed to his own groins. "We puncture the large arteries in the legs and put a small catheter in on both sides. You will be numbed up down there, so you will not feel anything but a needlestick and some pressure. Then using fluoroscopy, we advance a catheter that has a stent-graft compressed inside of it over a wire that we put up through the leg arteries. The graft has one limb attached to it, and I will deploy one end just below your renal arteries, and the other end will stop at the top of your right leg artery. Then I'll go up the other side and add a smaller limb stent-graft for blood flow down this side."

Dr. Michaels pointed to his left groin. "The puncture sites are closed with a stitching device called a Perclose ProGlide Suture-Mediated Closure System. It is composed of a plunger, handle, guidewire, and sheath. The device is designed to deliver a single suture or 'stitch' to close the puncture sites, 'access sites,' in large vessels in the leg, femoral vein or artery, following catheterization procedures. Perclose. The cool thing about this is you can be up and walking in four hours, then if you're good, you can go home the next day and back to work in a few days."

Jason said, "My god, why would anyone ever want to be cut open?"

Dr. Michaels laughed. "Not everyone can have an EVAR. Some would do better with an open repair. I feel like we could get a good outcome for you with the less invasive approach. What do you think?"

Jason answered, "I'm scared, Doc. What would happen if we just waited?"

Dr. Michaels responded, "Jason, it's probable that you would rupture at home or on the jobsite, and, buddy, if that happens, you can cancel Christmas."

Jason's wife was invited into the room and into the discussion. All agreed that the noninvasive procedure would be the appropriate one. Jason was prepared for the procedure which was planned to be done the next morning. No sense waiting. The mortality for ruptured AAA was extremely high; around 80 percent of women and 70 percent of men die after AAA rupture. Only a small percent make it to surgery.

It seemed clear that EVAR procedures would only increase in frequency. With the number of FDA-approved devices and the variety of modular device iterations available, practitioners were less often finding that open surgery was necessarily the better option. The bottom line was that EVAR was less invasive and better tolerated by patients although not without its dangers.

"We are ready for you in the CVOR [cardiovascular operating room], Dr. Michaels," the nurse said. The CVOR is a hybrid operating room like a standard OR but outfitted with digital fluoroscopy and computers where you can use a patient's existing CT scan and measure the anatomy using 3D reconstruction.

George Michaels was in the dressing room with his head bowed down, doing a combination of praying and going over the procedure for the umpteenth time in his mind. He has done plenty of these procedures and has yet to have any life-threatening complications. Thank the Lord. There has been occasional stumbling and speed bumps along the way, and the postoperative period is when leaks and kinks occur. Jason would need close continuous follow-up with CT scans. There was one post-op leak treated with embolization and some stumbling with the closure devise on the groin incisions. So that was it…

By the time Dr. Michaels walked into the operating room, Jason was already prepped and draped and was given a few milligrams of Versed by the nurse anesthetist. He was already snoring. The local representative for the AAA company, Chad, was already in the room.

Chad said, "Good morning, Dr. Michaels! Would you like to review my case plan?" The company reps played an important role in these procedures. "We love to have them here to support the procedure. They see so many cases and are well equipped to make suggestions that will help the procedure to go more smoothly."

Dr. Michaels said, "Sure, Chad, and thanks so much for being here on such short notice."

"No worries, sir," said Chad.

Chad brought the case plan up on his iPad and pointed out where the aneurysm started. It was about thirteen millimeter from the bottom of the lowest renal artery. "We must be careful not to deploy too high, otherwise we could cover that renal artery, and that would create serious problems for Jason." Chad also pointed out the common femoral artery measured only 7.2 millimeter in one area with a ton of calcium located at that spot. The catheter sheath that they would be using to access the artery is 18f (a little bigger around than a drinking straw). "We can try to get past that tight area in the common femoral with the sheath, or do you think we should dilate it with a balloon first, Dr. Michaels?"

Dr. Michaels said, "I don't think it will be a problem, so we'll just go for it."

Dr. Michaels thanked Chad again and left to go put a lead apron on and scrub his hands at the scrub sink. What's going through his mind at this point early in these pioneering decades? *Open versus intravascular treatment of abdominal aneurysms? Personally, I would go with the least invasive procedure. The mortality of an open procedure in an often very obese patient is at least 10 percent and probably higher in the hands of the typical surgeon covering a small-town emergency room… simply not prepared.*

George and Rex recently had this very conversation typifying the reason George pushed for EVAR. A sixty-five-year-old Caucasian lady presented to a community hospital with 3–4/10 back pain. She was just traveling through the town when the pain hit. On physical exam, she had a pulsatile abdominal mass. CT scan revealed a six- to seven-centimeter AAA. She was headed to see out-of-town relatives a considerable distance away that they couldn't make it in time for patient support. From out of town, passing through. She had no idea of where any hospital was in that town. She called 911 from her cell, very anxious and frightened, so shaky it was hard to find the numbers on the cell phone. Sirens blaring, they were ten minutes away.

An EMT responded when the GPS found her location. Because the pain was rapidly increasing, she was taken directly to the nearest hospital, a small community hospital of 250 beds. The general surgeon on the call schedule would recommend calling a vascular surgeon, but there was no vascular surgeon on their call list. It would take too long anyway; emergently there was no choice. Perhaps it's better to bleed to death at home while asleep oblivious of anything wrong in your belly. In attempting to get proximal control of the aorta, the aneurysm ruptured, and the patient exsanguinated.

Rex admitted that he would not put himself in that position ever again. "Refer this type of vascular catastrophe to the vascular surgeon on call. Don't call me. Get the unfortunate patient to a level 1 trauma center. George, you are even better with the free rupture headed in the right direction certainly with EVAR, and we small town general surgeons applaud you. There isn't any boatload of vascular surgeons interested in taking call in a small understaffed hospital's emergency room. Liability, too great in any emergency room for any doctor! But refusal to respond to the urgent call and hanging up the phone is unconscionable. If you are *it*, then you and prayer is all you got!"

*****

The following is the narrative of a case just being done on Josh by Dr. Michaels dictating as the procedure flows.

"Okay, so the procedure has begun. The patient has been prepped and draped in the usual fashion. As I was scrubbing in, my daughter suddenly popped into my mind, and I was wondering how she was doing. We haven't spoken in a week or so. As I walked into the room, my usual team, I called 'em the A-Team, was ready to go. I stepped up to the table looked at the patient's monitor, and he was in a normal sinus rhythm which is what I would expect. I asked for lidocaine which was handed to me, and I injected over the palpable groin vessels bilaterally. The areas in which I will be working were now numb. I use the fluoroscopy machine to look at both hips to locate where I would do my needlesticks if the femoral pulses were not palpable. I typically use an ultrasound-guided access to make certain I keep clear of any calcifications. The needle I first use is about three and a half inches long, advancing forward at an angle until under ultrasound, I see the needle enter the femoral artery—I shoot just a bit of contrast material to verify my position. I get immediate blood return and insert a guide wire through the needle lumen as I watch under fluoroscopy and move the wire into the aorta.

"I back the needle off the wire and insert and advance a catheter/sheath which will give me access through without allowing blood to leak out. We access both groins without issue. My local rep for EVAR is a guy by the name of Chad. We've done this procedure together probably a hundred times. He's a good guy, and we see each other at meetings a lot. He loves what he does, and he's confident and competent. I depend on him a lot to size from a CT scan, the correct measurements for the graft, and trust that he will let me know if there is anything unusual about the patient's anatomy. We work well together. I put what's called a pigtail catheter through the sheath in the right groin under fluoroscopy. I'm watching the catheter on the screen as I am putting it up through the femoral artery all the way up to where the renal arteries come off. It's especially important to keep the graft away from the renal arteries. It can create a big problem for these patients if we were to cover one or both arteries. Acute hemodialysis dependent renal failure from migration of the graft is one of the grave complications of the minimally invasive EVAR. Additionally, there is a 30 percent complication rate.

"My scrub technician, Mary B., attaches the pigtail catheter to our auto injector that is filled with contrast that allows me to see the renal arteries in the aorta real time. The live imaging is always so helpful. I step on the imaging pedal, the room lights dim, and I call out, 'Inject'! The contrast flows through the pigtail catheter, and the renal arteries light up right away, and the contrast flows down from there. I see this big aneurysm about a centimeter below the renal arteries that extends down to about five centimeters above the bifurcation of the iliac arteries.

"For this young patient, I choose not to do a cutdown on the right groin to put in this large device. The sheath I'll need to put in is 18 French, which is about size of your little finger. Just then I thought about a patient that I wished I would've done a cutdown on a few weeks ago. I think to myself this patient's much younger. I don't see a lot of calcium, and I think this will do fine. On these larger percutaneous procedures, I like to use a device that I call a 'magic stitch.' I backed the sheath out, and Mary removes it from the wire in the right groin. She then advances the first 'magic stitch' device, and I deploy it in the patient's groin. I now have a suture around the arteriotomy I created with a needle and the sheath earlier. I backed that delivery system out. Mary removed it from the wire and gave me a second device which I deployed with no issues at all.

"Chad is standing next to the monitor across from me with a laser pointer and a marker. He is marking the monitor where the renal arteries come off, so we won't put the graft anywhere near there. Mary is now removing the second magic stitch device, and I noticed the 18 French sheath in front of her. I look over, and the flush device is still open, so I reached over and closed it. I asked Chad again what size graft we are using, and he tells me that it is twenty-five millimeter, which I remembered from reviewing the case this morning with the team. Mary is now prepping the device behind me on the back table, and I turn around and watch her as I have so many times before. Why does my daughter keep coming to mind? I should be focusing on the case in front of me. I tell myself I need to call her after I get finished here.

"Mary says I have the graft ready, so I ask her to go ahead and load it on the wire, and she tells me to wait because we haven't put the sheath in yet. I realized that at this moment, I need to focus and stop thinking about Valerie. So Mary loads the sheath on the wire, and while she is doing that, she doesn't look up, and she says, 'Doctor, are you okay today?' I said, 'Yes, I'm fine, just have a lot on my mind.' She says—God bless her—'Let's buckle up and get this done!' Mary's always my voice of reason during these cases, and I think to myself, *God, thank You so much for having her here with me. She helps keep me calm, makes me laugh, and lets me know if, God forbid, I miss something.*

"So now I have the big 18 French sheath in. As it was going up, I'm thinking to myself, *Wow, that really felt crunchy as I was pushing it through the iliac artery and into the aorta.* And I'm thinking to myself, *It really didn't look that bad on the CT.* I then reached over to the left groin and asked Mary for a thin wall needle and stuck it into the groin to access the left common femoral artery. I advanced the wire up without any difficulty, removed the needle from the wire, and placed a smaller seven French sheath without any difficulty.

"I asked the anesthetist, Jose, how are we doing? Jose said that the patient was stable with a blood pressure 130/80, and we were good to go. I said, 'All right, Mary, let's go.' So Mary loaded the graft delivery system onto the wire, advancing into the sheath. It just felt a little tight as I was advancing it up, and I wondered again if I should have done a cutdown. God, please let this be okay. I'm watching the graft come out of the sheath into the aorta, and everything looks good. Chad says as he points to my fluoroscopy screen, trying to land it at the line I've drawn here under the left renal artery. So I advanced the graft up and placed it right on Chad's line. We're good to go. This device has a complicated handle delivery system to deploy or open the graft. It's kind of like a flower opening, so sometimes I must adjust a little to make certain that the top of the graft lands where I want it to go. This deployment was 'spot-on'! I go and manipulate the handle of the deployment system and continue to deploy the graft and then an extended limb down through the right femoral artery. Chad smiles and says perfect deployment. I remove the delivery system and start to focus on the patient's left groin. There is a little opening called the gate, and I must steer the guide wire into the gate and advance it up into the graft. Thank God I'm in, and this is going great.

"Mary has already got the limb prepped, and I ask her to advance it into the gate, and it deploys without a problem. Chad says, 'Perfect, let's check it with a pigtail and make sure we don't have any leaks.' So Mary loads the pigtail catheter in the right groin. Again I step on the pedal, the lights dim, and I say inject, and in front of me, I see a beautiful result with no leak, and I'm thinking, *We are home free*. I close my eyes thanking God for being with me and this patient, Josh! We may have celebrated a bit too soon.

"The last part of the case is closing the holes we have made in the groins' femoral arteries. Mary steps around me and is ready to hold pressure on this right groin, so when I take this huge sheath out, we don't bleed profusely from the groin. So I start to back the sheath out that is in the right groin, and Jose says from out of nowhere, 'What did you guys just do? We have a pressure of fifty.' I already had the sheath out and looked at the tip of the sheath and a piece of the artery was there. I said, 'God, help me!' Jose says, 'Come on, you guys, you have got to do something. The pressors aren't working. So I called out, 'Give me a twelve-millimeter balloon.' I knew what had happened. I knew we ruptured the right groin, and if we don't do something quick, this patient is going to die. I thought quickly about his family. I swallowed hard. I'm talking to myself, 'I've got to get a balloon from the left groin over to the right groin to stop the internal bleeding.' I yell at Mary to give me a balloon. I keep trying to steer the guide wire from the left groin over to the right groin, and I'm struggling. Jose keeps telling us, 'Guys, come on…' I'm sweating profusely and trying not to panic, closing my eyes again, and in my mind, I'm thinking, *Please, God, please help me*. Just then the wire travels down the right groin. 'Mary, where is that balloon?' Mary says, 'I have it! I have it!' Mary loads the balloon onto the wire, and I advance it up and over, and the balloon is inflated. We wait a few seconds, and Jose says, 'Whatever you did, his pressure now is back to normal. I know that this patient is going to make it off the table its working!'

Now that I have control, thank God, I can just do the cutdown that I should have done in the first place and patch the hole that we made when we removed the sheath. In my mind, I'm thinking to regroup, calm down, and do what I know to do and fix this. I've probably done a thousand groin cutdowns and endarterectomies in my career, and now I know the patient is going to make it. My Savior has once again saved and guided me and saved this patient."

(Searching the Internet for the early pioneering of this procedure, the history is quite detailed, and that history can be found at *Endovascular Today*. A full history is available there and begins with a discussion of the first AAA repair in 1951, and I thought those interested might enjoy reading it.)

*****

Josh had a quiet, uneventful post-op course, and because of the trouble with the right femoral artery having to be repaired, Josh was kept an extra day in hospital. George Michaels, after he was finished with the case, was going to head south after touching bases with Rex Swiss. He was praying that his beautiful young lady's faith would keep her safe. Valerie has known the Lord since grade school.

15

Lisa Michaels

Sometimes life seems like it's going out of control, and that deep inner thought is, *Did you hold on to Jesus?*

I'm pulling up to my first hospital of the day. It's an hour away from home, and it seems worlds away from where I really want to be. My truck is loaded with everything I need to have for any cardiac rhythm management (CRM) implant procedure. I've been a CRM rep for fifteen years now. We're on call at night and on some weekends, ready to see patients and provide service to our physician customers at the drop of a hat! To say that I'm attached to my cell phone and electronics is an understatement. Do other people panic when they can't find their phone after five minutes in their own home? It's just part of the CRM lifestyle. I know that it's really a privilege to be able to be so involved in the implant of these sophisticated devices. I love it most when I get to interact with patients and help to allay their fears about how their pacemaker works and what their life will be like with an automatic implantable cardiac defibrillator (AICD). It's life-changing and potentially lifesaving when someone has a lethal arrhythmia like ventricular tachycardia. People are so afraid, and rightfully so, about the procedure and then about what life is like afterward. I know it's God's grace that has given me this privileged opportunity, but it is so demanding and distracting. My husband's career is even more demanding, and it has been a strain over the years, but we've figured it out for the most part that we are a great team [sic].

So here I am, pulling into the hospital's parking lot for my first encounter of the day, and I think, *Will we do this for the rest of our lives?* People would kill to have our careers…so why am I so reflective today? There is something just unsettling in my soul today. Deep in my soul, I feel like the Lord is leading me toward a different type of healing career. Whatever it is, I don't know now, but I will follow His lead. I hop out of the truck, albeit a lot slower these days.

The physical demands of this job are beginning to wear on me. I check my product bags to make sure that it's loaded with anything that the doctor might need for the procedure. I carry two of everything and then some. As I am dragging two large bags across the parking lot, I joke with a passing stranger that I feel like I'm in CrossFit training. Everyone that I see either says, "Hey, are you moving in?" or, "You could fit a couple of bodies in those bags!" It's true, the bags are heavy and strain my tired, injured body.

I finally make it into the procedure room. It's kind of a funny little family. I've known some of the staff for over fifteen years. It's time for all of us to set up and take our places for the next patient. I find my usual spot on the opposite side of the cold hard table where the doctor will be working. Unfortunately, my spot is always behind a huge bank of monitors. All the patient's vital statistics are displayed on the screen. The C-arm is in position, and the images are displayed on those monitors as well. It allows the doctor and everyone in the room to see what we are placing inside the patient's body. I just wish that this hospital has a monitor on the back of this system so I could see what's happening without running around the room to the side the doctor operates from.

I link my programmer and the integrated pacing system analyzer (PSA). It's my responsibility to test the wires that are placed inside the patient's heart. I also must let the physician know if he is in a good place with good signals and that's necessary through those leads in the patient's heart. I'm in position now behind the monitors and begin my work.

Why in the world is my phone blowing up again? Don't they know I'm in a case with Dr. Impossible, I mean Dr. Incredible… incredibly impossible—that's it! Group messages drive me crazy. I know my team. "The team" of six in this territory are all working hard in their respective locations today, we need to communicate real time…all the time, so I know group text messaging is vital to manage the day, but it's just one of a list of many things driving me crazy.

I've already scanned the product to make sure that it's safe to implant. I just need to get started programming the device to Dr. I's preferences. Certainly, he is bound to change a few things. I've already studied this sweet little lady's chart, and she has some very unusual arrhythmias. Oh, sorry, what was that you said, Dr. I? Sorry, sir, I can't hear above these monitors or see for that matter. Let me just run around the room to your right shoulder so I can hear you better…careful don't get too close to the sterile field. Oh, you want the music on? Okay. What are you in the mood for today, sir? A little hip-hop? Oh, okay, 'Ariana Grande' it is! Good Lord, help me! Isn't he a grown man? One second, sir, let me just get back to my phone… the one I left blowing up my programmer behind the monitors.

I know "the team" can clearly see on the schedule that I'm in this case and that I'm not carrying the pager for "the team" this week… wait a minute, am I? Oh crap, what is Dr. Impossible yelling for now? I see twenty-five text messages on my phone and have a sinking feeling. How is that even possible in two minutes?

First things first, find the right music for Dr. I. Okay, music on streaming from my phone, deep breath. Today we're doing a BiVentricular AICD. He's getting access now in the patient's subclavian vein three sticks, three sheaths… Oh crap, did the scrub tech put the correct size sheaths on the sterile field? Let me just run around the monitors to the sterile table one more time before I try to catch up on these texts. Candace is scrubbing today with Dr. I. I can always count on Candace to be spot-on. Yes! Thank you, Jesus, Candace is on it. They have everything they need!

These cases can be challenging even in the best of situations, and with Candace by his side, I can rest a little easier. I'm behind the monitors once again and have a few minutes to hide and find out what is going on with twenty-five text messages! Oh, good, only eight from "the team"? I just assumed they were all work related. Oh nice, a few from our daughter Valerie and one from her boyfriend as well. That's a bit odd. It's not often I hear from him via text. Valerie is an amazing young woman and absolutely living a blessed life. Her boyfriend is so perfectly suited for her. I smile a little inside me and my mask that they both texted me today. Let me just get through "the team" text messages first; there may be something urgent happening. I'm feeling some anxiety rising in my spirit, or is it just this case? Pushing that thought aside, I do a quick scan, and it seems like everything is covered from a team standpoint. I just need to see a patient upstairs when I'm finished with this procedure… Lord, please don't let me forget to see this patient. Dr. I has all three sheaths in now. I have the device programmed…well, for the most part anyway. Now I just must be sure shock therapies are disabled before I hand off the device so no one gets hurt. I check myself on that point at least one hundred times in every case. Where is this anxiety coming from? Dr. I has placed the first lead in the right ventricle…pay attention, Lisa!

To make matters worse, it's EVAR Tuesday. My husband is a territory manager for a medical device company that makes heart valves. They are implanted in a unique way through a catheter in the groin. It's incredibly complex, something I know I could never do in a million years, nor would I want to. Tuesdays are the days when his schedule is completely overloaded with these complex and very often risky procedures. I'm honestly not even sure what hospital or even what city he's in today! I always hesitate to call him on these days.

I finally get a break just as I receive another text message from Keith, and he seems upset. He tells me the situation with Valerie and that surgery is mandatory because of a life-threatening abdominal catastrophe. Dr. Swiss wants to operate right away. Right about then, Michael calls me to let me know that he has talked with Dr. Swiss and trusts his judgment, and that he agrees with the surgery and tells Dr. Swiss that they will be praying for all concerned and they will head in their direction.

Today, I didn't hesitate a nanosecond. He picks up almost before the phone had a chance to register a ring. "I'm on my way there!"

I respond, "Me too. I'll call you from the truck."

I've packed my massive bags, the ones that carry "everything I could possible need" for every procedure and struggle down the long hallways of the hospital. The weight of these bags seems heavier every day. My body burns and aches with every step. All I can think of is getting in the truck and speeding toward Valerie. I must talk to my husband… I'm running to the exit of the hospital when I suddenly remember, I have a patient to see on the floor! Dear God, can't we just lead a simpler life? It's about to get more intense.

I pause in the lobby of the hospital and make one phone call to my work partner Matthew. I know when I explain to him that I have an emergency regarding Valerie, he will make sure our patient on the floor is seen by someone else.

He hears the panic in my voice and tells me, "Go, do whatever you have to do! I will be praying for you all and your daughter!"

With every single step toward my vehicle, I pray with every fiber of my being the most powerful prayer I can muster, "Jesus, Jesus, Jesus."

With every step, I called his name and nothing but his name, Jesus, Jesus, Jesus!

Tossing my bags in the truck, I dive behind the steering wheel and call my husband.

When he answers, I can feel his heart is breaking, but miraculously he has the doctor on the phone, and he conferences me in. Our worst fears are confirmed. Our daughter is in a life-threatening situation. She needs emergency surgery. Without it, she has no chance of surviving! The surgeon seemed confident, caring, but very concerned. He said they were setting up the operating room for her now, and if we had no further questions, he needed to go.

We are at a complete and utter loss! We begin problem-solving; it's in our nature. We keep going over and over the possible logistics just to get there. We have a rough idea of our plans. There are so many phone calls to make. Calls to the airlines, calls to neighbors to look in on the house, calls to friends to take care of the dogs. I'm suddenly struck—the most important call is for us to call on God! Why do we forget and leave him out? I know my husband prays but not usually out loud, so I ask, "Honey, before we go any further, we need to call on God," and without hesitation, he says, "Yes, of course!"

Lisa's plea to the Lord and his throne of grace, "Father God, you are good, and we praise you now and forever. We love you and trust your promises. Your plans are not to harm us but to give us a hope and a future. You love us with an immeasurable love, so much so that you sent your son to be sacrificed to pay for the sins of the world. Through his sacrifice, you overcame death, and you promised that by his wounds, we are healed! Father God, Lord of all, protect our daughter, heal her by miracle or by modern medicine. Guide the hands, hearts, and minds of the physicians and entire medical team. Father God, let nothing pass from their attention! Let the presence of your Holy Spirit rest on us and our family and bring us peace that passes all understanding. We thank you and we pray in Jesus's name. Amen."

My husband is working in a city that's closer to Valerie, and it only makes sense for him to drive. There were no flights available that would get us there more quickly, so we both have to make the drive. He'll arrive before me but not by much.

At moments in life like this, what does the believer do automatically and consciously, its second nature to him. It's like if one sees another vehicle just seconds before a head-on collision and you have no escape, the God-shaped part of your soul only God can fill that causes a reflex, believer, or unbeliever, and we cry out the name of Jesus or God to help us. You simply have no control over that. You might say that at this last second, if you have at least that, you can't help but cry out to Jesus. We all are made in the image of God. We are having our last communion, our deathbed confession. Your soul cries out, you have no control over this, and you call on Jesus. It began with your first breath as your soul entered your body. You cry out to your Father, to the One who created you to save you. O dear unbeliever, he has wanted you to ask for his help all through your life, and you were a blindman. You couldn't see it. At the time of Jesus's death on the cross (Luke 23:46), Jesus called out with a loud voice, "Father, into your hands, I commit my spirit." When he had said this, he breathed his last. If God gives you another moment, you will cry out, "O, my God!" or "O, my Lord," and he hears that. I'm reminded that Peter could walk on water until he took his eyes off

Jesus. Hopefully, he does give you that final second so that you could cry out to him and claim that he really is your God. He died for the entirety of the world's sin.

That is what Lisa was doing, and that was not only the only thing she could do. At the same time, it was the very best thing that she could ever do—calling out to Jesus. God hears what's in our heart. Lisa's great testimony to her deep faith in Christ is evident. But when he saw the wind, he was afraid, and beginning to sink, he cried out, "Lord, save me." Jesus *immediately* reached out his hand and took hold of him, saying to him, "O you of little faith, why did you doubt?" And when they got into the boat, the wind ceased. And those in the boat worshiped him, saying, "Truly you are the Son of God."

16

Valerie Michaels is a twenty-year-old Caucasian female presenting to the emergency room of the Teaching Hospital with an eighteen-hour history of crampy, mid abdominal, periumbilical pain with nausea, vomiting (fecal) and bloating. No prior history of abdominal problems, no recent change in bowel habits, no fever or chills, no weight change. Normal menstrual history. The pain was 10/10, causing her to "double-over" when the pain occurs. She was quite anxious and fearful in acute distress. "If you don't do something, I am going to die. Please help me!" Negative pregnancy test (for completeness). Dr. Mullen caught Dr. Swiss who was evaluating another patient and asked him to see Valerie Michaels. On exam:

A thin crying twenty-year-old Caucasian female presented acutely ill, frightful. Temp 99 P100 rr10 with shallow breathing (splinting), bent over holding her distended abdomen and vomiting of fecal-smelling gastric material. The onset was several hours after a gymnastics class at college. Abdomen distended and tender around the umbilicus, dull to percussion with absent bowel sounds. Nasogastric tube was placed with a resultant quick liter of fecal-smelling aspirate to empty the stomach before she is put to sleep. Flat and upright abdominal films prior to CT of abdomen revealed multiple loops of distended, fluid-filled loops of proximal small bowel. CT scan consistent with a distal small bowel obstruction. Foley catheter placed with clear but concentrated urine.

Valerie was seen by Dr. Swiss at the request of Dr. Mullen. After his evaluation, Dr. Swiss was able to have a brief conference call with George and Lisa, alerting them of the situation just before taking Valerie to the operating room with preoperative diagnosis of distal small-bowel obstruction, etiology to be determined. Dr. Swiss could be seen in the locker room on his knees, head down with tears in his eyes, lifting Valerie up to the throne of grace. A very tough decision but he had no choice. If the bowel was strangulated, it could die along with the patient. Because of the urgency and marked distention of the abdomen, this patient underwent an exploratory laparotomy through a midline incision. (Laparoscopy was felt to be inappropriate in this patient's case.)

Findings revealed a twist of the mid to distal distended bowel around a Meckel's diverticulum beneath the umbilicus. The small-bowel proximal was hyperemic, slightly thickened and viable without evidence of ischemia. With release of the obstruction, small bowel slowly showed peristalsis. The Meckel's diverticulum was sharply detached from the undersurface of the umbilicus and excised with a stapler across its base.

(The diverticulum is a vestigial remnant of the omphalomesenteric duct. It is the most common malformation of the gastrointestinal tract and is present in approximately 2 percent of the population containing two types of cells, gastric and/or pancreatic cells.)

Valerie's parents were contacted by Dr. Swiss when the patient was taken to the PACU awake and alert with little complaints related to incisional pain but much better with a different kind of pain, manageable. Her boyfriend, Keith, was allowed to see her for just a few moments. Both parents were headed to the hospital three hundred miles apart at different hospitals after Dr. Rex Smith assured them that Valerie was going to be all right so and to please be careful getting here to be with her. Valerie is in the postanesthesia care unit, awake and alert. Her abdomen is no longer as distended as it was before the surgery. She is much more comfortable and thankful. Most Meckel's diverticula are asymptomatic and just an incidental finding which really needs not be removed unless, as it was with Valerie's case, it was the cause of her obstruction. George and Lisa Michael's are en route!

Interesting etiology to Valerie's presentation…after gymnastics exercises. Could there be any gymnastics movement/exercise that might cause the small bowel to wrap around a Meckel's diverticulum attached to the undersurface of the anterior abdominal wall?

Meckel's diverticulum is described by the "Rule of Twos," which states:

- It occurs in 2 percent of the population.
- The symptoms usually appear before the age of two or within the first two decades of life.

There are two types of ectopic tissue (gastric and pancreatic). It is usually located within two feet of the small and large intestine junction (ileocecal valve). It is approximately two inches (five centimeters) long. It is two times more likely to be symptomatic in males than females, and 2 percent become symptomatic.

Based on Valerie's subjective and objective presentation, it was entirely proper (if not lifesaving) that Rex Swiss wasted no time in operating on Valerie. One could envision so many complications had he not operated in a timely fashion: With a stomach massively filled with feculent liquid, she could have vomited and, as a result, developed aspiration pneumonia; the small bowel could have suffered ischemia and become gangrenous and perforated causing peritonitis. She could have become septic, and all that entails hypotension included. I believe this occurred as a direct result from a gymnastic move with the Meckel's attached to the umbilical undersurface and freely moving normal small bowel around the fixed point! (I have seen it.)

17

What happens to us in the first minute after we die? Do we enter heaven immediately, or do our souls go into a sleep until the end of time when our souls and our bodies will be reunited? I've always had lots of questions about heaven.

The Bible doesn't answer all our questions about heaven and life after death—and the reason is because our minds are limited, and heaven is far too glorious for us to understand. Someday, all our questions will be answered—but not yet. As the apostle Paul wrote, "Now I know in part; then I shall know fully" (1 Corinthians 13:12). (Perhaps we will fully know God's Word, the greatest story ever told.)

However, the Bible certainly does indicate that when we die, we enter immediately into God's presence if we belong to Christ. From our earthly point of view, death looks somewhat like sleep—but not from God's point of view. Paul declared, "We are confident (of eternal life), I say, and would prefer to be away from the body and at home with the Lord" (2 Corinthians 5:8). Elsewhere he wrote, "I desire to depart and be with Christ, which is better by far" (Philippians 1:23).

Later, we will be given new bodies—bodies that will never age or be subject to death because they will be like Christ's resurrection body. As the Bible says, "The dead will be raised imperishable, and we will be changed" (1 Corinthians 15:52).

> Is your hope in Christ? Death is a reality—but so is God's offer of salvation in Christ. Don't put off your decision for Him, because you could be called into eternity at any moment—and then it will be too late. (Billy Graham)

But what about Sgt. KW Wayne who slipped and fell in the hallway of the VH some three months ago and now essentially is in a vegetative state? Prior to his trauma, he has always professed that he was a child of God. That down in history, he is a faithful member of a family of believers. His eyes are open now as he seems to scan something we will probably never be privy to on this side of the Jordan River.

He has aged well in strength and good health. When Moses and Joshua died, they were also enjoying health but time to move on according to God's plan. "Moses was a hundred and twenty years old when he died, yet his eyes were not weak, and his vitality had not diminished" (Deuteronomy 34:7). God buried Moses, but no one knows where, therefore, no vigils to that spot. God's plan.

God probably kept Moses's gravesite secret because he knew the Israelites had tendency to place worship in wrong places and things. They needed no diversion in the forty years of wandering. They did not need one more distraction to keep them from entering the Holy Land. Joshua was 110 years old when he died. Sergeant Wayne was like Moses in a way...his mind still functioning especially when it came to long-term memory...still alive nearing one hundred.

Several years ago now when stronger, KW wrote a *long note* about the year 1968–1969, a year in the combat zone as a combat infantry soldier in the Republic of South Vietnam. From draft notice till touchdown on USA soil, he remembered it well when he wrote for the book in 2020.

*****

Three strikes and you are in? Not part of the indoctrination was the appendectomy first, then driving a truck for Sears and then the draft notice, the trifecta, I *was* in! This was followed by a whirlwind of adventure over forty weeks, the army making me a trained killer, a sergeant squad leader. But you know the most important event in my life happened the week before the trip to Vietnam. I got baptized in the name of the Father and the Son and the Holy Spirit, immersed like in the Bible! I honestly believed that I now wore a shield of honor and strength. I knew in my heart and soul that I was ready emotionally and spiritually.

Eighteen hours over water, refueling somewhere in Japan and then landing at Tan Son Nhut AFB outside of Saigon and getting my wakeup call, marching by flag-draped coffins of heroes going home. I learned quickly to hate war but hated the enemy more. Those who were survivors wore the once green uniforms like mine, theirs is now mud-cake brown. Proud survivors of twelve months and I was just starting. They were going home, something they had hoped and dreamed for and prayed for. I had no idea as to what lie ahead for me, and all they wanted to do was forget twelve months of their lives. I'm sure thanking God all the way the long journey home, the USA. I cherished the small Bible that I kept every day in my army uniform front pocket.

But first, welcome to my new home, 199th Light Infantry Brigade, near a town called Long Bien, also serving and protecting another small town called Ben Whoa. Our mission, our base of operations protecting Saigon's east and northeast. At sundown, we were welcomed by the unbearable heat that I would live in. At a large building, officers and noncoms drew gear first—weapons, ammo, grenades, bayonets, and camouflaged uniforms. We were assigned a platoon and a squad of twelve men I'd never met before who would have to trust in me to make it alive at the end of twelve months. Six of the men had already seen combat and the other six just fresh off the plane that carried them here. Those veterans having seen combat, I made it a point not to tell them how to fight... I just wanted to learn. We were all just grunts or ground pounders. The following 5:00 a.m., we woke for breakfast and loaded up in trucks to carry us thirty minutes away. We were told to "lock and load," for the enemy could be just around the corner, and to remain vigilant at all times. Then we found out where the trucks were taking us. It was unexpected and unbelievable. We were taken to a Bob Hope and Connie Stevens USO show along with more GIs than I could count. Was this a dream? Did I make this fantasy up in my mind? It didn't last long enough, and we were back at base camp, locked and loaded. It all was happening too fast.

We were back in the trucks headed out. Those who had been here a short while, even those of lower rank than I, could read the fear and uncertainty on my twenty-one-year-old face. No way to hide it at that point. I got up off my seat and went over and sat down between two of them and said this, "I need your help." I said to the veterans of combat, "I will only give you one order. Help me keep these six men alive for as long as you have remaining in the NAM, show us what you've learned, and if I made a mistake, just tell me, and I will accept and respect your criticism." We all bonded that day!

We arrived at the outpost camp surrounded by artillery guns, men on the perimeter and helicopter gunships. NCOs and officers hustled into a large concrete bunker to be welcomed and to receive info and maps. Carried the info to my squad to "prepare them for the mission we were about to go on. Scary times! Who slept that night? I certainly didn't. Lost a lot of sleep that year." I was called "Shake and Baked," an instant NCO simply because I became a sergeant in eight months when it took years for others. As you can see, squad leaders were killed rather quickly in the NAM, so the army had to develop an intense training course to replace them.

Transport helicopters arrived early the next day, and it was time to assemble the men, my men! Men? These were all frightened boys wondering what lie ahead. Their squad leader was just as frightened. I had at the very least to pretend that I wasn't afraid so these boys would follow me. We loaded onto the choppers and headed out to an unknown area in the Vietnam jungle. Our mission that day was to make contact with the enemy and get "body count," which simply meant kill some of these men we never met before or knew anything about. Did they come from good families? Did they have children? Were they religious? Who were these soldiers, and were they as scared as we were?

Whenever the choppers touched ground, we would run and form a circular protective area around the choppers to protect it from gunfire. When the choppers and the gunships took off, we were on our own, young, inexperienced men all alone. We would head out into the jungle unaware of what lay ahead. (This was a whole lot different than playing army with my brothers in Stemmer's Run behind Grandma Becker's house in Baltimore, Maryland, in the early 1950s.)

My squad was second squad. We were to follow behind first squad that very first day into the mission. Our mission was to last seven days. After the seven days, our lieutenant would designate an LZ (landing zone) for pick up. The LZ was always in an area of the jungle, wide enough for the helicopters to land, load our men on, and take off. This was a very dangerous time because (Charlie), Viet Cong would hear the choppers arriving in and set up an ambush to get as much body count as they could. Dangerous times in the pilot's and crews' lives. None of us were safe at any time. We were all in our Lord's hands.

As first squad moved out, cutting our way through the dense jungle was an exceedingly difficult task on every mission. We had to endure the thorns, snakes, mosquitoes, monsoons, and enemy fire, not to mention malaria. Not a fun time or a good place for a family vacation. No one was looking forward to this mission. We moved about two clicks into the jungle when all of a sudden, rapid-fire was heard just to the front of our position. As in training, we all hit the dirt. The lieutenant who was with first squad came running back and told my squad to face to our right and open fire. Apparently, we had walked into a Viet Cong Base Camp. Three of first squad's men had been injured. Kenny Leonard was critical, shot on the left side of his head. He was walking point when all hell broke out. Juan Pizzaro was wounded in his left arm, and Blair Olsen wounded in the right side of his leg. We had to get these men to an LZ and back to the rear for treatment in our makeshift hospital or naval ship… Welcome to the Nam!

As we were on our way to the LZ, we came under fire again. I and one of my men were carrying Kenny on a liter when the bullets started flying. We dropped the liter to hit the dirt. I have never forgotten dropping this severely wounded fellow soldier. He had a severe head wound, and Doc did his best to stop the bleeding. We didn't have an IV. There was really nothing that we could do but to try to get him medevacked so they could start treating this young soldier. The firing stopped. We got up and began the journey again. *Could we get him there in time?* was on all our minds. The two wounded men, Juan and Blair, were in no danger of dying now.

We finally reached the LZ, the chopper approached, but it was receiving heavy fire from Charlie. They had to go around and try again to land. We noticed where the fire was coming from and concentrated our return fire in that direction. The lieutenant radioed the chopper to attempt another landing. As the pilot came in, we thank God there was no fire from the enemy. The chopper landed, and we loaded our wounded. As the chopper took off, we were ordered to go back into the area we had just left. We all wanted to get on that ship and get the heck out of here. Our orders came from the rear, higher-up officers. Were they crazy or what? We had to obey orders or be court-martialed.

It was my squad's turn to lead the advance back where we had just had three men wounded. We were ordered to attack the enemy's base camp. I told one of my men to take point, but he refused. I asked another to take point. Both said that they would rather reenlist than to go back in there, suicide mission! I took point myself. When you go to the NAM or any war zone for that matter, you ever make it through and go back home wearing a brand-new uniform or leave in a brand-new body bag. It was certainly up to God.

Not wanting my men to see fear from me, we made it to the base camp. The enemy had scrammed (De De Mal) we called it. I entered one of the bunkers, and there was still steam coming from a pot of rice they were cooking. Lying on a small makeshift table was a small homemade cup with a wire handle. I still have that cup to this day. There was also an underground hospital full of instruments from China, Korea, and some as well as American in origin. I sent some of those instruments back home to my brother Jack who became a general surgeon following his educational journey. Proud of him today (as he types this remembrance.)

There are many more stories I could write about during my tour of duty in Vietnam. I wasn't wounded, thank God, but I did have malaria twice. You see, most of the time, I was in the boonies, and it was difficult to get the quinine medication to us, so malaria was inevitable. Many times, Doc would pull leeches off us after we crossed filthy infested rivers.

I made it home, and as I was walking through international airport, I saw people with signs pointing at me in my newly decorated army uniform calling out, "Baby Killer" or "GI Go Home," and "Murderer." They just didn't understand what I had been through over the last twelve months. Sad times in my military career defending freedom and this wonderful country. I would have gone again if needed.

Kenny Leonard passed away on the way to a hospital ship. I've often wondered, *If my wonderful brother Jack had been there as he came in, attempting to do all that he possibly do, could he have saved him?* God bless my brother Jack and brother David who also served with honor during a most difficult time in American history. Both men who refused to take point that horrible day reenlisted when we were pulled out of the jungle later that week.

My life could be sliced into two segments that I was forced to struggle with and endure. After my year in Vietnam, I struggled that 58,000 men and women gave their lives for a people they did not know and the war itself that was titled a *conflict*.

Juxtaposed with WWII, where there were parades across the country, veterans leaving their transport ships onto American soil with so many classic pictures of the emotionally reunited men and women embracing and kissing their heroes of a "real war." We Vietnam veterans were not welcomed home with any real emotion except distain for having survived a *conflict* that America did not approve of or support. Yes, many years later, we finally were acknowledged and welcomed home.

The Vietnam Veterans Memorial on the National Mall pays tribute to the brave members of the US Armed Forces who fought in the Vietnam War and were killed or missing in action. The memorial consists of three separate parts: The Three Soldiers statue, the Vietnam Women's Memorial, and the Vietnam Veterans Memorial Wall, also known as The Wall That Heals, which is the most popular feature.

If you visit DC, you will come across veterans still dressed in that eras clothing, in wheelchairs with tears in their eyes, flags attached to their wheelchair. Regalia of the forgotten veterans many with PTSD, they are still back in Vietnam because they were never welcomed home. They relive their combat experience as they look for friends and family searching for the name of their loved ones on The Wall. How were they thanked for their service? By suffering from the poison, they weren't aware of, that they smelled and felt and breathed and tasted everyday while in-country, Agent Orange. WWII veterans didn't have to go through the daily poisoning of all our troops. Did they ever test animals with Agent Orange before releasing it, or were we the guinea pigs? As it turned out, we soldiers were the mice and rats totally unaware of the horror we had to face in that country with constant poison in the air. The list of ramifications of Agent Orange is never-ending. The Veterans Hospitals and clinics deal graciously with the injured Agent Orange survivor, learning more about the poisons effects in the decades to follow the end of the conflict. From our standpoint, it is never-ending. Nightmares are common. Every system in the body is affected.

Agent Orange was a powerful herbicide used by US military forces during the Vietnam War to eliminate forest cover and crops for North Vietnamese and Viet Cong troops. The US program, codenamed Operation Ranch Hand, sprayed more than twenty million gallons of various herbicides over Vietnam, Cambodia, and Laos from 1961 to 1971. Agent Orange, which contained the deadly chemical dioxin, was the most commonly used herbicide. It was later proven to cause serious health issues—including cancer, birth defects, rashes and severe psychological and neurological problems—among the Vietnamese people as well as among returning US servicemen and their families.

Ole Sarg, he could spin some yearn anytime he could have an audience...sometimes just one person would do the trick. He gave lectures about how to stay alive in the bush. Sometimes he would go on talking with no one around. It was as if he had an invisible stenographer taking it down word for word. He would say things now fifty years later that he would never have said post-Vietnam. His age and mild infirmities seemed to afford him carte blanche to tell of the fear of everyday life, living in the enemies' front porch for everyday was a blank page of life being doused with Agent Orange, smelling it, tasting it, and absorbing it through both lungs and through the gut. Of course, finding out much later that they were poisoning him slowly, a little every day, and they were ignorant of the facts until much later. (Should the vaccine for COVID-19 have been tested on living animals before releasing it to the general population? Was Agent Orange given to rats or guinea pigs to see the affect before poisoning everyone? Remember thalidomide?)

His stories are in the book that we talk about, a compendium of stories both of war and of peace. Fresh pages to let it all out and over with. Held back for five decades. Now an old man…he was safe. They can't send him back ever again. He talks of yesterday as if it really were yesterday. He lived in the enemy's home turf. Vividly he remembered it all…held it in all those years. "Had to always sit with my back to the wall," still does. It was Bro Rabbits briar patch in Uncle Remus's stories, the Cong and they all looked the same, enemy or friend. They had us at a great disadvantage being in the briars. It was all about the jungle and body counts. You could not anticipate when they might appear. Much of the time, you just hear ricocheting of bullets and a general direction of where the sound was coming from. Or you could simply *bump* into them or occasionally trip over their bodies.

LZ? Be quick and low, don't forget the perimeter in spite of heavy enemy fire straight ahead. Can't land yet, not secure. The LZ was not secured yet, so we were told to jump out several feet above because of a heavy, steady rain for a full week. We jumped out, and immediately I was up to my waist in the ground saturated with rice water. I was the first one to jump. Didn't expect it, the flooded rice paddy. The pilot enjoyed the view laughing, might as well—can't dance! We were drenched and would stay sopping wet the whole seven days. No dry clothes. Our bodies were as the tips of our fingers when held under water, wrinkled constantly until the rains were stayed and the sun's heat at 105 degrees reappeared as it always did. Don't really know which was worse. We were hung out to dry, might just as well be in the dryer spinning around.

We had been in the jungle for about four days when we came to a large hill just in front of us. The lieutenant told me to take a few men and go up to the top of this hill and let them know what we found. "See anything?" I told my men to stand down, lie down in this water. It was even that way at the top of the hill. What did we find? Pay dirt! Thirty yards away from our position, a Viet Cong squad sitting around a makeshift fire, heating up their lunch. By radio, the lieutenant said to stay there, that he would pull both squads up alongside of us. When we were all in line and in position, he told me to yell "dung lai," Vietnam for *halt*. As soon as I said that, the Viet Cong grabbed their weapons, started firing, and took off through some low brush in front. We opened fire all across the line. When it was over, three of the Cong were dead. One was running toward a village, so we had to hold off firing our weapons. Innocent villagers or Cong (collateral damage) or civilian innocence.

We gathered up their equipment; there were maps and ammo as well as photographs probably of their loved ones. When we came back to base, two things came up.

First, the young villagers, some teenaged women, they were in every place—you name it—to entertain. The trucks that carried the entertainers from their village to the NCO club and safely back home after the club had closed needed ready guards on board, guarding their young women (children really). All over the globe, wherever you find the GI. The girls are there in Japan, Hong Kong, the Philippines, the girls were always there. Then I met the entertainer, Mylon. She was crying because her boyfriend was to leave the following day. They were saying their goodbyes, very emotional, almost comedic. Going home to the USA. After he said goodbye to her and they had parted, she asked me if I would be her new minoy! I met her family at her village and couldn't understand their gibberish. It was all about safety for the girls so they could entertain the troops starved for anything to get their minds off the war they were living in for twelve months. Watered down liquor for the grunt and Coke for the girls. She eventually asked me to take her home to America. Woah! There, gal, no way that's going to happen. No thanks. I'll be taking plenty back with me, thanks to Agent Orange. But I often wonder the fate of Mylon. Did she and her family survive the war?

Did she fulfill her dream of coming to America? I only knew her for a few weeks before I made it safely home.

Several months before going home, back to civilization, I heard about "Getting an Early Out"! There was such a thing? Are you certain? My brother Jack was back home in college after himself getting an early out. Between the two of us and angels, it might just happen. Not just a dream. He got the necessary enrollment papers for FTU, now UCF. It was just in existence for a year or so, and they were obliging. We got me some inside people to make it legally, truly happen. A month before I was scheduled to go home, it was all tied into a beautiful package in yellow ribbons. I was accepted, a reality I could not have prayed for. I was out. Flying back home early!

Veteran of a *war*, we didn't win and took the lives of fifty-eight thousand men and women for something they were ordered to do by many who have never even flown over that country; some to this day couldn't point out on a map the location of that country that took so much and gave us poison day in and day out. That terrible war zone, a war never really understood except by those who lived it and fought in it.

Yet many protested it and, yes, even downplayed and humiliated those of us who served, fought, and died.

Our troops were certainly not welcomed home until decades later. Finally!

The Vietnam Veterans Memorial on the National Mall pays tribute to the brave members of the US Armed Forces who fought in the Vietnam War and were killed or missing in action. The memorial consists of three separate parts: The Three Soldiers statue, the Vietnam Women's Memorial, and the Vietnam Veterans Memorial Wall, also known as The Wall That Heals, which is the most popular feature.

The Vietnam Veterans Memorial Wall provides one of the National Mall's most powerful scenes. In truth, the *wall* is actually made up of two identical walls that each stretch 246 feet and 9 inches, containing more than 58,000 names. The names are listed in chronological order based on the date of casualty, and within each day, names are shown in alphabetical order.

Perhaps the memorial wall's most defining characteristic is a visitor's ability to see his or her reflection at the same time as the engraved names, connecting the past and the present like few other monuments can. If you wish to spot the name of a relative or friend while there, search the Vietnam Veterans Memorial Fund's Virtual Wall before you embark or find the on-site list.

Just south of the Vietnam Veterans Memorial Wall is the Vietnam Women's Memorial, which commemorates the 265,000 women who served in the Vietnam War, many of whom worked as nurses. The two-thousand-pound bronze structure stands fifteen feet tall and depicts three women attending to a wounded soldier, reflecting the unity required during the conflict.

The third part of the Vietnam Veterans Memorial is The Three Soldiers (also known as The Three Servicemen) bronze statue, another moving reminder of the disparate groups that had to come together during the Vietnam War. Each of the three soldiers stands seven feet tall, situated on top of a one-foot granite base, and are arranged as if to show the three soldiers gazing upon the memorial wall at the names of their fellow comrades.

Honoring Veterans

On any given visit, you may encounter former servicemen at the memorial. In fact, the Honor Flight Network is a nonprofit dedicated to bringing vets, often elderly, to DC to visit the memorials which honor their service to the nation. These visits are often filled with emotions and help provide closure for veterans by reinforcing the importance of their service and sacrifice.

Only Jesus knew why I was there and placed his arms around me and whispered, "All will be well, my child, have faith," and he was right.

I said that there were two phases of my post-Vietnam life. A doctor of chiropractic! Four years of undergraduate studies at UCF and four years of graduate studies at Palmer College of Chiropractic in Davenport, Iowa, a small town I had never heard of before. I had to look the town up on a map to find out how to plan an automobile trip there. I wanted to study how I could help others who had difficulty with certain health conditions, who suffered daily with pain.

What was really in my future once again?

I didn't know that eventually following graduation from that college in Iowa that I would be faced with the same attitude from those who had no idea what they were talking about, responses from others remarkably similar to post-Vietnam public disdain. Following the initial setup of my practice, I thought to practice in my hometown and that I would be welcomed. I knew a lot of people in the City Beautiful, I grew up there. Boy, was I wrong! I would hand out business cards and flyers and introduce myself as Dr. Weitzel. When asked what kind of doctor I was, I would say that I was a chiropractor. Most of the time, the responses were not flattering. "Oh, you aren't a real doctor" or "I went once, and they didn't help me." How could I not be real? I breathe, I go to church, and I eat, sleep, and dream. What's not real? I studied for eight years of my life to make my life and the lives of others better. Service to patients who are in pain is not being a real doctor? Back on their depression meds I suppose. PTSD is bad enough, now I'm not a real doctor?

Men and woman who fought in World War I, World War II, The Korean Conflict, the war in Iraq and the war in Afghanistan were all given a warm "welcome home" almost immediately upon exiting from planes or ships.

It took more than twenty years for us Vietnam Vets to be *eligible* for a "welcome home". Sad but true…but received with a grateful thanks from deserving men and woman long forgotten and certainly overdue!

I tell you, if my faith and belief in Jesus Christ wasn't an integral part of the parental nurturing in my life, I would have joined those men who died in Vietnam a long time ago.

I'll pick up the rest of the story from what KW told me, his brother. It was as if we were on a merry go round, and it didn't stop until he retired from his miraculous chiropractic career. Education degree, Palmer School of *backaching* just as his license tag says, "Backache." Can you imagine or grasp what an active practice as a chiropractor for twenty years is? The number's too many to count.

Patients are grateful for his God-given talent and a heart as big as all outdoors.

Then he was a one man show for seniors for many years, delivering meals on wheels for more than nine years, giving gallons of blood, guitar-picking entertainer of the years gone by in the lives of extended care facilities residents. Certainly the seniors greatly appreciated KW, but Sergeant Doc KW had to do it, for it was in his genes. His parents showed that it was better to give than to receive.

How it all began in his words: Many years ago, I was delivering meals on wheels to a nursing home facility when I heard some music coming from one of the large rooms off the hallway. As I approached the doorway, I saw a husband and wife playing the piano and singing to a small group of men and women in wheelchairs. It appeared that those in the audience were having the time of their lives, clapping, singing along, and enjoying life if only for a while. I listened for a while, but I had some more stops to make. As I was driving to the next meal recipient, I kept thinking about how beautiful that scene was and how thoughtful that man and woman were to take the time to visit that nursing home and provide some small form of love to these forgotten souls. I looked, but I didn't see any family members or visitors, just staff and those living there. So sad!

I said to myself, "I want to do this. I want to add some small form of sunshine to the residents who I'm certain look forward to anything other than eating, sleeping, and missing life on the outside." I played with the guitar during quite times in Vietnam. I guess it started my desire to share with these nearly forgotten. I loved playing the guitar and could somewhat fake a few songs on the piano. So…I went straight to work, practicing songs for months that I knew these folks would know from the twenties, thirties, the forties, and yes, even songs from the fifties and sixties that I knew from my day. I was ready to give it a whirl. Along with an eight-by-ten photo I presented myself at a very small, assisted living home. I approached the manager and handed her the paperwork, and I said, "If you're interested, give me a call." The paperwork included a brief history of the songs that I would perform and my experience with music. I said, "At first, the entertainment would not cost the home anything, but if they enjoyed what they had heard and wished for me to return at some point, there might be a very modest charge."

About a week later, I received a phone call from the manager of that home, asking me if I could come and play for them in a few days. It was one of the residents' birthday—eighty-five years old, I believe—and some music would be nice for the occasion. Well, I was elated and thought perhaps this was the beginning for me to give some sort of thanks to the Lord for what he had provided me all these years, especially surviving a year in Vietnam.

I arrived early, was given directions where to go, and set up the equipment. There were some residents already in that room, anticipating the birthday party, was anxious to meet this very nervous entertainer, and to see "what type of music" he would be playing for them…rock and roll, rap, or instrumental? Little did they know that it would be an hour of memories and songs they grew up with. After the hour was over, I didn't get a standing ovation, but the men and women in those wheelchairs yelled and clapped so loud that a few staff members opened the door to see what was going on with this usually quiet group. Such a memory for me and for them. The following day, the director called me back and asked me if I could come once a week and play for them. This weekly show lasted eight years. Unbelievable!

There was an annual meeting of assisted living and nursing executives at a large hotel downtown. Word got around, and I was invited to perform along with other entertainers. This was an audition for many of the homes that invited entertainers to perform for them. This was a way to get to know the talent in the area. This is where it all began. Some of the homes enjoyed my songs and invited me to come once a week and play for their residents. For many years, I enjoyed twenty-five to thirty shows a month.

They loved him, Sgt. Dr. Bobby Wayne. He once played a song, "Hey Good Looking." The lyric in the song has the phrase, "I got a hot rod Ford, and a two-dollar bill." In a totally near shocking moment, one of the elderly gals stood up in the joyous crowd and presented KW with a new-looking $2 bill. He never forgot that gesture and framed the $2 bill for his music room. But he gives the credit to where it is due, his Lord and Savior Jesus Christ, and yes, he was going to go to Disney World as soon as it opened in future years to come. "Walt Disney died in 1966, and Walt Disney World was opened in his honor on October 1, 1971, two or three years after I got out. It was as if Florida Technological University opened just in time for my brother Jack and me."

KW could always be seen with his portable chiro table in the back seat going *to* the patient. An added *gift* in his life was being the owner of his own airplane and his coveted pilot's license. He was thrilled to let our dad Charlie take control of the plane, climbing slowly toward heaven. Weren't they afraid? They were too crazy and having too much fun. Dad could barely see over the steering wheel to know where he was going. Charlie was a believer and had a near-death experience while playing golf. He knew heaven would someday be home, and he never feared death. In the end, he welcomed it, suffering from end-stage heart disease and a chronic leukemia. He, once at the kitchen table, visibly depressed, stated, "I don't know why I'm still here."

Three weeks before Chuck passed, KW tells of the situation. "I remember taking Dad to his doctor's appointment. He was being treated for chronic lymphocytic leukemia. He had been very tired and depressed that day on the way to the office. He was holding his head down most of the short trip and wasn't really saying much. I tried to talk to him, but his answers were brief. It took a lot of effort to speak. After we arrived at the doctor's office, we checked in and had a seat in the waiting room. Dad immediately assumed a head down position and was looking around at all the other patients waiting their turn with the doctor. He looked at me with these very intense eyes, and I asked him if there was something he wanted to say. I didn't expect his answer. With a shallow voice and a small tear running down his cheek, he simply said, "KW, I can't do this anymore. I just want to go home and get in bed and stay there." I said, "What, Dad?" He said, "It's my time!"

I stood up and went over to the reception window and asked if I could speak with the doctor for just one minute. I was escorted to the hallway and met his oncologist. It was difficult for me to get the words out without crying myself. I managed to say that Dad was ready to "give up." He doesn't want to come here anymore or take any medication or treatment. I asked the doctor if he could order hospice for our family and, if so, could I take my dad home and give him his wishes. We went home that day. Dad undressed, got into bed, and stayed there.

Hospice came soon to evaluate the family's needs and worked with us those final two weeks. Of course, Mom was in denial, saying that he just needed to start eating and he would be just fine. We assembled most of the family and stayed with Dad until Jesus met him a short few days later.

As his time on earth was coming to a close, he welcomed death. He finally just ran out of life, out of gas! He had *nothing* to do! He had *no*where to go! He turned inward; the closer death approached. (This was in 1997, somewhat before the PC age, perhaps on the cuff. If he had a PC, something to occupy his mind, he might have lingered a bit longer, perhaps another six months, but in the end, boredom and starvation took his life. Yes, he gave up, but he had heaven on his mind, and he told us that.) In the end, he finally touched heaven, now in spirit, better than in a Cessna!

That's where this chapter ends with Sgt. Dr. KW Wayne touching heaven at ninety-two years young, just his time as it will be with you. Will you one day touch heaven? "Life is but a *vapor,*" says James, the half brother of Jesus. In James 4:14, it says that life is "even a vapor that appears for a little time and then vanishes away." Our time, no matter how you chose to spend it, is over quickly.

Are you ready like KW?

18

Ever since Paula discovered the cryptic note taped to the window of Central Supply, she had made her concerns known to the administration. She is becoming more anxious daily. Who made the puzzled, jumbled note, and why? She constantly ruminates. Initially a Wednesday visit with her psychiatrist might calm the fight or flight Paula is faced with. This was getting serious because Paula has now been off her medications for three weeks for what was diagnosed several years ago as PTSD. The drug acts to regulate neurotransmitters in the brain.

The chief of staff administrator at VH is the only one who even knows Paula is a psychiatric patient or what her weekly Wednesday afternoon activities are. You can be certain the puzzled note to Paula, though seemingly anonymous, highly suggests to Paula of who wrote it. Why would that be or rather who would that be?

Paula, at first, was ambivalent regarding her early afternoon appointment that Wednesday. They seemed to do no good, and she was embarrassed that she had stopped taking what has been a stabilizing drug for years for her. Stopping that medication and not seeing her doctor. (Beeper goes off every Wednesday directly after the office visit at 2:30 p.m.) Sondra once again did not want to deal with the emotional roller coaster of her life. She had thought of suicide so many times, but what little faith now having essentially left her, there was no buffer to turn to. In addition to her diagnosis of PTSD, she also has DID. Treatment has been hypnosis and "talk therapy." After the appointment Wednesday, she intended to go to the Teaching Hospital in Fledgling, find the wife of Dr. Adams, a pediatric surgeon, and tell her of their platonic Wednesday affair.

This information would disturb and disrupt their lives enough for the moment. She had to get to Celeste.

She had been given a beeper to communicate as needed. One never knows when this signal will go off. The fact that she had a means to communicate if necessary was a relief. Like clockwork, Wednesdays were rather etched in stone when her DID came to the front. (As you will recall, Paula's parents and twelve-year-old brother were killed in a horrendous accident when Paula and her twin sister Laura were ten years old. Both girls had significant injuries requiring lifesaving surgery and lengthy rehabilitation. They were raised separately.) Paula had been to counseling and under the care of a psychiatrist ever since, known only to the chief of staff, Dr. Brice Adams. It was believed without doubt the accident at ten years of age had been the catalyst, PTSD, causing her psychiatric problems of so many years. (The dissociative identity disorder is the sequelae of all this. What just happened?)

Paula becomes Sondra with a total changeover after the office visit at 2:30 p.m. The presence of two or more distinct identities or personality states, each with its own relatively enduring pattern of perceiving, relating to, and thinking about the environment and self. At least two of these identities recurrently take control of the person's behavior. Inability to recall important personal information that is too extensive to be explained by ordinary forgetfulness. The disturbance is not due to the direct physiological effects of a substance or general medical condition.

At the last moment, amid tears and trembling, she would be late but had to talk ASAP. She headed to the four-lane. Looking at the vehicle's speedometer, she was going too fast and frankly couldn't focus because of the tears. She entered the interstate, and from behind, she felt the typical "NASCAR nudge" on her right rear bumper. Immediately, there was no time for a thought from Sondra, for during one of the rolls, she was ejected through the driver's side left windshield. At the speed she had been traveling, she entered the slower right lane and was "accidently tapped" by a vehicle in that lane going at a higher rate of speed. There were other vehicles surrounding her. Most managed to avoid involvement, but several vehicles made it quite an accident scene, though only Sondra and the driver of the van were injured. Did anyone see what had happened? (Pileups happen in every NASCAR race, and only rarely is anyone seriously injured. They have the luxury of videotape to diagnose nearly perfectly who did what and to whom. After clearing the track, the race nearly always continues as drivers knocked out of the race are looking for someone to blame while the pit crew tries to make their vehicle drivable. Nor are they thrown from a vehicle. They are strapped securely in their vehicles. Very, very few injuries as a result.)

Sondra wasn't wearing any seat belt. Here we have nothing except the possibility that a white van may have initially been involved. It also was involved in the accident with major front-end damage. The driver, who was in shock with left upper arm fracture and blunt abdominal trauma, was taken by ambulance to the Veterans Hospital. It was at his wish to go where he was known and respected, and then he lost consciousness.

One driver trailing was behind a white van, but it all happened so fast they did not see any advertisement on the side of the van nor a driver. Perhaps many of the drivers were thanking God they were not injured. We would hope they would thank him even though they otherwise barely ever thought of their Creator and Sustainer and even now will not give him a second thought.

An ambulance arrived. Sondra was unconscious, not moving.

The ambulance crew, always on standby within eight minutes, placed Sondra on the stretcher. Rapidly assessed, this was a deadly scenario. The vehicle didn't resemble a vehicle. The driver, unrestrained, was ejected through the window and lay a few yards away. A trauma alert was issued from the ambulance to the Trauma Institute of a rollover on the four lane: middle-aged Caucasian female patient, barely breathing, unconscious, blood pressure 80/120 heart rate, pupils dilated but not fixed. The ambulance was at the Trauma Institute within ten minutes. She had been intubated quickly on the way to the institute. The monitor showed the pulse slowing down. They got Sondra ready for the CT scan of the head, neck, and chest. This scanning device was like the x-ray checkpoints at the airport. This was a dynamic study of the total body showing any bony fractures and dynamically showing active bleeding from solid organs, spleen, liver, and more all within two and a half minutes. A large bore IV catheter placed. Multiple lacerations with obvious upper and lower extremity fractures. Blood was begun. The CT scan revealed marked swelling of the brain with intracerebral bleeding.

Transplant service was notified of a possible donor. There was no identification on her person. The mangled vehicle was searched, and apparently her purse with identification was found. Driver's license showed the vital information of Sondra Barnes. Other than that, it had extremely limited information. Sondra's vital signs were stabilizing on the ventilator, and there appeared there was no trauma to her chest and heart, but she was considered brain-dead. Multiple upper and lower extremity fractures with soft-tissue blood loss. She was moved to the transplant side of the institute and readied as a heart donor. Victims of vehicular accidents with certified brain death are always candidates for organ procurement and without the need for permission. It has been a law on the books for going on fifteen years. There still are long lists for prayerfully waiting recipients.

*****

Brice Adams was the driver of a white leased van only driven on Wednesdays; otherwise, it was kept in his garage. This was strictly accidental, for what Brice wanted to do was to get Sondra's attention to comfort her through this episode so that she would reconsider telling Celeste and breaking up his marriage. "You can't possibly do that on the interstate with the speed limit of seventy miles per hour." This van suffered significant front-end damage, and driver's side window was damaged but intact. As the EMTs were carefully extracting Brice from the vehicle, he was briefly awake long enough to tell them to take him to the Veterans Hospital and then lost consciousness. They failed to radio ahead to brief the emergency room of the situation, the apparently dire situation. The ambulance was there in eight minutes. On arrival, the personnel were in shock but not as much as their beloved chief of staff. You could hear a chorus of "Well, I'll be damned" and "Oh my god."

After being closed for the past two months as a cautionary measure, it appeared that Dr. Adams would be the first to open the swinging doors to the suite. OR personnel were already at work setting up for anesthesia and the surgical back table. Someone said to get the pack wrapped in red cloth for emergencies such as this. Anesthesia was very thankful to be back to work until they realized who the patient was but had to not think of that but to do their thing.

Dr. JD Tucker was the general surgeon on call, and they were ready for him when he arrived in just a few minutes. Dr. Tucker looked carefully around the room and at anesthesia who gave him a thumbs-up reassurance of his readiness. Brice had been infused with the ERs uncross matched two units, and four units were in the process of being ready. Dr. Tucker was telling everyone, "Get all the lap pads you can. As soon as we open, his pressure will drop further. We'll need to scoop out all the blood and clotted blood and pack everything off until we find the bleeding point." Tucker made the typical tried and true midline xiphoid to pubis incision. After being able to see the situation, it appeared that the spleen lay in pieces with its blood vessels actively bleeding. Appropriate control was gained, and vessels ligated with heavy silk stick ties. As he was receiving the fourth unit of blood, his blood pressure was beginning to normalize. The incision was closed with heavy Ethicon sutures in the fascia and retention sutures. He was not waking up from the anesthesia, so he was kept intubated on the ventilator and moved directly to the PACU, going through the swinging doors where Celeste and Laura were prepared, hugging and holding hands tightly. All were waiting to see how Brice was doing and to let him know that they were there.

Brice's wife had been notified and was extremely upset over the situation and not thinking straight. She needed and sought the help of her dear friend, Laura Hunter, director of nursing at the Teaching Hospital. Laura gladly took over and drove Celeste Adams to the Veterans Hospital. They arrived just as Brice was being brought out of surgery and taken to the PACU. He was starting to wake up from the anesthesia. Celeste and Laura were standing one on each side of the bed as he awoke. Obviously oblivious to the events of the past two hours, he woke briefly, long enough to see the two women by his bed and then looked from one to the other and on the ventilator. He couldn't speak but was wide-eyed and anxious and was needing sedation, not ready to be extubated.

The nurse caring for her husband appraised her of what had happened…she was told to wait in the surgical waiting area and the Dr. would be right out. Celeste was frightened for her husband's life. She was fortunate to have Laura's friendship. They had grown accustomed to seeing each other every day; it couldn't be helped for their offices were right next to each other. The two of them shared their inner thoughts, and as weeks and months went by, they became best friends.

They enjoyed coming to work every morning. Rarely were they apart. It had been rumored by some that they were gay. Celeste had a relationship with the Lord, and knowing right from wrong, she relied more on her relationship with Laura than her faith. It seemed to have begun as Celeste would speak of her faith trying to witness to her friend. Laura pretended to go along with Celeste's world view, but it was an act for Laura, stealing her attention away from her faith with more reliance on Laura. You see, Laura would do anything and everything to have the love of Celeste Adams, even to the point of pretending to believe what she believed. It was easy for Laura who could be anything that would please Celeste even to the point of faking a relationship with the Lord of the universe. It was like spitting in the face of God.

If Celeste would speak of her relationship with Christ, Laura would cringe inside herself. When Celeste tried to share her faith with her friend, it was easy to fake holiness. She occasionally was asked to go to church with Celeste and always had an excuse. The closer she got to Laura, the further Celeste got away from her faith. Celeste really was an easy prey as the enemy used tragedy; Celeste was defenseless. She was not at all aware of the armor of God, she had no shield of faith, no helmet of salvation, she had quit praying, and her Bible unopened. Celeste stepped into the enemy's camp and had no breastplate of righteousness, no belt of truth only friendship with the enemy. Satan was pleased. Once again, he won the battle using light and beauty and self-love. He convinced Celeste, truly a babe in the faith, easily swayed by her surroundings, and her faith faltered and fell. He had won!

Dr. Tucker assured Celeste that surgery went well and what they had found. The only problem was that he was not waking up after the anesthesia was over. He had probably had a concussion, and they would get a CT exam of the brain, but he was certain that he would be fine. They also mentioned that an orthopedic surgeon would check out the left humeral fracture, but everything else was stable. There were also left lower rib fractures nondisplaced, which was good, but they would keep his lungs expanded because he wasn't yet breathing deeply enough on his own.

Brice's blood pressure was slowly rising to symptomatic levels and a decrease in his heart rate. Suddenly he had a grand mal seizure, which was treated with IV Dilantin. After which, it appeared that his right arm and right leg were not moving, but there was posturing highly suggestive of a subdural hematoma. A neurology consult was requested while the patient underwent an emergency CT scan of the brain. This was consistent with a left-sided subdural hematoma. An acute subdural hematoma (SDH) is a clot of blood that develops between the surface of the brain and the dura mater, the brain's tough outer covering, usually due to stretching and tearing of veins on the brain's surface. These veins rupture when a head injury suddenly jolts or shakes the brain. If there is a significant delay in diagnosis and treatment, the mortality rate is just over 50 percent. Advanced age increases the mortality rate as well as with patients on blood-thinning medication.

Neurology confirmed the diagnosis, and a neurosurgeon drained this through a burr hole. Hopefully and prayerfully done, it would take time to see the results. After the surgery, there was no change in his symptoms and signs suggesting there had been perhaps a long enough delay that damage might be irreversible. There now is a 60 percent mortality rate. Brice is holding his own while Celeste was with the family in the second-floor chapel, praying. At this point, it appeared that an arm and leg exam suggested permanent damage from the unrelieved pressure on the left side of the brain. If there were a rebleed, he might not be able to recover from this.

19

And then it happened! Brice opened his eyes; he moved all four extremities normally, except for the fractured arm, and was breathing well enough with stable vital signs. It was unbelievable. Brice tried to remove his endotracheal tube, and a quick reexam by a startled neurosurgeon and a nod to the medical team, Brice was extubated and was able to speak and understand perfectly well. He had trouble with the fractured humerus, and orthopedics decided to treat this nonoperatively by a hanging cast. (The fracture was later reduced and was stable without surgery.) You know what he said with a nasogastric tube in his nose? "When can I get something to eat?" This comes but less than twenty-four hours from lifesaving abdominal surgery and successful surgical relief of the subdural hematoma. Incredible and miraculous!

Celeste tried to convince everyone that this was a miracle and an answer to the prayers of the righteous! Celeste, not being known as a Christian, in fact, only God knew her spiritual condition. This was so acute and so acutely relieved that everything fell back into place. I guess! No one had guts enough to challenge her on the praying! Keeping him comfortable, not letting his blood pressure rise again and sedating him, watching closely for blood to reaccumulate. Celeste stayed in the waiting room. The next day, he was transferred to a private room, the NG tube removed, and he tolerated clear liquids. Finally, he spoke and thought that he remembered Paula being in the room. Was he hallucinating because of drugs? Celeste was by his side. He was discharged on day 5 in perfect condition after a near-fatal accident. He might very well or as easily rebled and even died. As he and Celeste left the hospital, everyone walking behind this miracle could do nothing more than shake their heads in disbelief. Perhaps someone would take a step closer to faith in prayer and faith in Jesus Christ. Laura was in the crowd of onlookers. He saw her but said nothing. He would swear that he saw Sondra or Paula.

However miraculous his recovery, on the sixth day, he began to have fever to 101 at first, then up to 102. He developed nausea and was no longer tolerating his diet. He vomited, and fear struck him and the staff when he began complaining of left upper quadrant pain radiating to his left shoulder and developed a cough. A stat CT scan of the chest, abdomen, and pelvis was done. There was evidence of an accumulation of fluid in the base of the left lower chest as well as left lower lobe atelectasis.

There was evidence of a large left upper quadrant abscess developing where the spleen had been removed. This scenario had been played out before with the post-op infections from the surgical schedule. In fact, nearly identical. But the surgical suite had been closed for some time, so this single emergency stood alone. While he was still in the radiology department and after everyone's opinion, it was decided to let them insert a drainage tube. Immediately purulent material was aspirated, and of course, Brice had gone through the mill and had left little reserve to fight this abscess and pneumonia. He was begun on total parenteral nutrition but was behind the eight ball. Celeste believed that he would recover from this through their prayers. She chatted with one of her distraught friends who had confided that perhaps there was some truth in the miraculous but now wavered with this unforeseen development. They set up a prayer chain across the country.

After twenty-hour hours of being unconscious, the fevers dissipated. He dreamed that he had seen Sondra.

Using the incentive inspirator, he was taking better, deeper breaths and coughing trying to beat the pneumonia. They were beginning to hope things were turning around, and it took about a week, but once again, he was without fever for forty-eight hours and hungry. Believe it or not, this all resolved, except for why did it happen?

*****

M & M Conference on the ensuing Saturday, much time was spent discussing the events at the Veterans Hospital. It seemed to be a real question of sabotage with tampering of contaminated unsterile instrument packs. It had to be this. Someone had used the original material from Sgt. Pat Poley's perirectal abscess. The only question remained was who and how was this carried out. Brice's abscess post-splenectomy mirrored the same bacterial spectrum as the previous double-digit patients had.

Head of Central Supply Paula Hunter had not been seen or heard from since Brice's near-fatal accident on the interstate. She had been rather secretive regarding her life outside the VH. In fact, no one had a clue of where she was and why she would walk away from this at this time. Was she afraid someone would accuse her of carrying out this sabotage? Whatever family they could find had lost contact with her and were just as concerned. She had an aunt, but her parents and brother had been killed in a fatal auto accident when she was ten years old.

As Brice was improving now quickly, he could think enough to contribute his thoughts about the debacle. Everyone had their opinion, and Austin spoke up curious as to Paula's activity every Wednesday, once sacrosanct. When Brice heard this, it occurred to him, although he had to keep it to himself, that it was also strange that Sondra was only available on Wednesday afternoons. She had a standing appointment with a psychiatrist Wednesday afternoons. But Paula and Sondra were certainly not two peas in a pod. Brice knew them both he thought very well; of course, he was mistaken but could not see it. Had Paula had anything to do with these suspicious post-op complications?

Brice had no means of communicating with Sondra. It would be a couple weeks until he was well enough to visit the golf course. No one had seen her. They were aware of the events surrounding the accident and were surprised that Sondra had not been there to ask someone about Brice's condition. In fact, she had never returned to the course from that time onward.

Answers were needed and not forthcoming. Paula and Sondra indeed were being seen by psychiatrist(s). Was it just coincidental? Sondra had never told Brice which doctor she was seeing before meeting him at the golf course. When questioned, the VH had no record of the name of Paula's doctor, nor did anyone working with her, only that it would be Wednesday for sure. She made it a point that she was not to be disturbed on Wednesdays after lunch.

20

There has always been a monumental international supply and demand issue with regards to tissue transplantation particularly with end-stage solid organ failure. Regardless of mass media getting the issue before the public, there are social issues improving but still inadequate research. The supply of solid organs had been improved with the no permission brain-dead trauma patients offering up those vital organs. Although the liberal society such as the ACLU turned that into a great social argument, we are making further progress. Tradition is just that, the way it's always been.

This reality has created the need for completely new therapeutic alternatives for the management of end-stage organ disease. What is needed is some way to bridge the gap between an ever-increasing need and a response, supply, not ever able to keep up with. It's been that way for decades, especially in the era of generations getting healthier and aging well.

Beginning with the postmodern shift at first with the baby boomer generation to each subsequent one such as Generation X and the millennials. Should we be going in the direction of mechanical device improvement both in using long-term application and more ease of usefulness? Yes, we have stopgaps but never long enough. No one should have to go through three dialysis treatments a week. It should be a Vas Cath, three dialysis sessions, and then a living kidney.

Looks from the literature that we are headed in two directions although there will always be traditional transplantation. The great desire of the 2010–2020 years was really to eliminate dialysis. Kidneys should always be available, and there are ways to make that a possibility; some will never be accepted by the public who have no interest in scientific issues until faced with the horrors up close and personal. Let them see a busy dialysis unit to see how tremendously burdening it is with these desperately ill patients. Give death row inmates the opportunity to give back a life that they have wasted or, further, a life they have taken. If there is diabetes, hypertension, tobacco addiction, obesity, and other comorbid conditions, there will be a need for continued research. On the other hand, a different progress was underway in transplantation. Kidney and heart transplantation saves and prolongs human life.

The new development is in what is called composite tissue transplantation. The terrible facial trauma leaving gross deformity of the facial structures, the burden of not being about to have children because of a lifesaving Caesarean section for massive bleeding, transplantation of composite tissue, uterus, and face. Facial transplant surgery is accomplished to overcome such problems. Uterus transplantation is emerging as an alternative to female infertility. Transplantation of composite tissue includes different organs. The main purpose of composite tissue transplantation is to restore reduced or completely lost functions and to increase the quality of life. Nerve regeneration must occur because of transplant to regain sensory and motor functions. It appears that the future of transplantation involves developments in two main avenues—invention of completely new tools for solid organ transplantation and advances in the transplantation of different organs including uterus, face, and composite tissue. Consider heart transplantation using the similar dimensioned porcine heart. We have been using porcine grafts with success with heart valves for as long as we can remember.

Twenty-two-year-old Caucasian Melissa Dixon has been in the Transplant Institute being monitored for three weeks. Dad and Mom have hardly left their daughter's side. When told that there was a possible donor heart, she couldn't speak because she was on the ventilator, but she was awake enough to shake her head to let them know she was a go. The family knew Melissa could not hold on much longer. She was born with a congenital cardiac anatomical defect and was operated when she was but thirteen. She had stabilized with slowly worsening ventricular function, but the heart function eventually deteriorated to the point that nothing short of a heart transplant would extend her young life. A heart transplant had been prayed about for years. This was the beauty of the institute.

Samantha proceeded with opening of Sondra's chest while her fellow, Dr. James Renfro (husband), readied Melissa in the adjoining operating room. Communication was always ongoing between operating rooms. James encountered some difficulty getting into Melissa's chest because of previous median sternotomy and some bleeding taking down the adhesions beneath the sternum. With Melissa's baggy, enlarged worthless heart removed, it appeared as a perfect fit in her empty chest. Immediately after a shock, a normal sinus rhythm was seen on the monitor's screen and a huge sigh of relief followed by light applause as Melissa's chest was being closed.

In the post-op recovery room, Melissa was waking up. She had tubes and wires seemingly everywhere, and she was gently told what each was for by the nursing staff.

Sondra's kidneys were likewise harvested, and calls went out to possible recipients. Both kidneys were flown out to other transplant centers in need elsewhere. The endotracheal tube was not new to Melissa, and she wouldn't have to keep it much longer. After a couple of hours with her wide awake and somewhat fighting the ventilator, the breathing tube was removed. There were other drainage tubes which would stay in for several days. Melissa's parents were thrilled to see her tube out, and she able to talk again, stating that she could definitely feel stronger.

*****

We now have more mystery, and it has become a matter for the police department/highway patrol in New Fledgling as well as for the VH. Somehow, these events of the past several weeks were so bizarre they must be related. There is someone responsible for all of this, and they must make a mistake to be found out. Thus far, what do we have? We have ten plus counts of attempted manslaughter and an interstate accident leading to the death of a Sondra Barnes and the stable but critically ill chief of staff, Dr. Brice Adams, now in the SICU post-op lifesaving laparotomy. Mildred's death more than likely was an accidental opioid overdose and not related (although there was no autopsy done, not allowed by the family).

To this point, it appears that no one thought of or spoke up about CS and OR cameras. They are usually on in the evening hours after the surgical schedule has been completed. When the crew leaves, almost religiously someone will turn on the cameras and review every tape of the main camera in the entrance to the OR. The automatic doors will swing open, welcoming anyone on the job or for some mischief perhaps. There is nothing on any of the camera's history over the past two months. If you spend the time looking more closely at the tapes every hour of the two months, what would you see? Thievery was the main reason for the cameras—purses being stolen, individuals there who have bad intentions.

Approximately 720 hours of camera surveillance, twelve hours times sixty days. We were looking for a needle in a haystack. Precisely a half hour here and a half hour there, 1/720 hours = 0.001, but they did not know even that, so they were literally lost with respect to the camera surveillance in the surgical suite and in Central Supply. There must be a mistake somewhere. This just shouldn't be. Someone sat with the camera's tape in their hands, and there was absolutely nothing but a blank 720 hours of boredom. (Unfortunately, had they been more observant to detail, they could have noticed the position of the long silver back table, the table that was moved around to CS to deposit the tainted wrapped trays of instruments upon. There was no way to roll that table to the exact position by room 1. Had they compared frames [weeks apart], they would have noticed on tape that the position was off by about two inches, and the camera would have picked that up.)

Who do we know who would be in the business of multiple counts of attempted murder? What possible reason/motive, and why those patients? It is as if a game is being played with human lives. Whoever did this, what were their intentions? Did they believe they were possibly killing these anonymous individuals? Or not? Thank God there were only the sergeant and Mildred fatally wounded. The sergeant was at the proverbial last straw who nearly killed himself waiting if he had and not taking care of his own health and, Mildred, an accidental overdose of opioids which she probably shouldn't have had ordered at all in her fragile state of health. That order should never have been given and worst-case scenario with her comorbid diagnoses age of seventy with COPD, a pacemaker and still smoking. In retrospect, Mildred would probably have fared better without the surgery or at least should have been kept overnight. Likely the coughing destroyed the sphincteroplasty, but no one will know without a postmortem exam.

At this point, we have no clue as to motive, just even numbered rooms and odd numbered rooms. This person is a hateful individual and for what reason other than insanity and he or she is likely to strike again, so the surgical suite is closed for now. Attempted homicide brings the local authorities in to assist the VH staff, police in the building and on the interstate. How are these related and what about a white van with no markings or advertisements? There, of course, are the white vans of the laundry service which are in the hospital's parking lot six or seven days a week. They have the logo of the laundry company on both sides of the van, the white van. Are the logos removable? Yes, they are magnetic. But they are still in the parking lot of the Veterans Hospital, so that's going nowhere! They aren't damaged.

21

Many years ago now, though no one recalls what year it was when Milton Conover was a bright, highly recruited twenty-five-year-old black man invited to interviews at an Ivy League medical college. He was tested by a psychologist and found to be at the genius level. His brother Delbert was eighteen months younger. Delbert also was a genius with a PhD in physics. There was a junior college about thirty minutes away where Professor Conover taught introduction to physics and basic chemistry.

Milton had a brilliant career ahead, the first black man of the Conover family to graduate from college in the late twentieth century. Delbert could have taught at any four-year college, but due to his brother's needs, he was subservient to those needs and became Milton's transportation. The first two years Milton excelled in every course biochemistry, gross anatomy and physiology, pharmacology, physical diagnosis, genetics, endocrinology, introduction to clinical medicine, and diseases and therapy.

Just as he was beginning his junior clerkship year, he complained of a severe headache and was found to have a blood pressure of 240/130 with difficulty with his vision and speech. He was quickly seen by an emergency room physician and given the diagnosis of malignant hypertension.

With the importance of malignant hypertension diagnosis lies in the fact that if untreated or if treatment is excessively delayed a poor prognosis (likely outcome of an illness) rate sets in. Often this will result in a five-year survival rate of only 1 percent of diagnosed patients. This means most patients will not make it beyond one, two, three, or five-year marks.

MS3 Conover had a stroke involving the right side of the brain with left upper and lower extremity weakness and vision loss in one eye. He was not thinking clearly either, placed in the ICU with a nitroprusside drip and pain medication for the headache. His family was notified, and for the next twelve months, he underwent intensive physical and psychological therapy.

He was maintained on heavy-duty antihypertensive medications. The successful therapy was a result of his desire to excel, to continue his great future, which was not to be. He was left with weakness in the left arm and a limp. Several years went by, and he found himself struggling with alcohol and drug dependency. He came to the Veterans Hospital and was hired as a janitor/orderly. He was brought to work by his caregiver his younger brother by eighteen months. He made his schedule to allow Milton to be driven to work and picked up on his way home. They had done this now for many years. His brother would do anything and everything to care for Milton.

One afternoon, Milton was helping a patient into their family vehicle when a middle-aged obese man was passing in front of him. Suddenly the man clutched his chest in agonizing pain and collapsed right in front of Mr. Conover. Milton bent over the gentleman and felt for a pulse. When none was palpable, he made a fist with his two hands together and suddenly hit the man in the chest. He began giving him mouth-to-mouth resuscitation. He felt for a pulse and felt a thready carotid pulse while by now the code blue team arrived, hooked the man to the monitor, and he was noted to have ventricular fibrillation. He was intubated, and his heart was shocked, and he began to be somewhat wakening. Placed on a stretcher, he was taken to the cardiac care unit with now a normal EKG with evidence of some ischemia. Milton became an instant hero. And as his job as a janitor, he had been reassigned now permanently to the second floor where the critical care units were, the surgical suite, and Central Supply. He has access to everything on this critical floor.

Milton doesn't talk much with anyone, for his speech is somewhat difficult to understand, but he's no dummy. He is a fly on the wall in the second-floor critical care units. When all this was happening, of course, he was quizzed as to anything he might have seen. Since it appears everything was happening late at night, probably nothing happened during Milton's work schedule. If something unusual were to happen, it wouldn't get past him.

There were times—a few, not many—when Milton was asked to work late into the night only in this capacity as a semi-security guard on the second floor. Professor Conover was concerned that Milton had never been in the security business and did not like much the idea of so late at night. It was always on a Sunday when he would come in late just for a few hours. There had been times when the pathologist was doing a post in the absence of the morgue diener. He was Washington's backup, very rarely, as well. He enjoyed those special times outside the lines. We know that Milton had to take several weeks away from work because of depression. We aren't privy to his depression battle, and we shouldn't really be concerned with that fact. Unless does his depression put him as far back as having to give up his medical career because of the untimely stroke in his junior year of medical school. Does he remain bitter as a result, and at times, that bitterness could have led to retaliating against the medical profession, to be off the edge mentally? Was that a possibility? Very doubtful.

Except to say that it seems quite coincidental that the nights that Milton was called to duty as a security person were on Sunday evenings. In fact, if you looked at the schedule log, you would see that Milton was on the watch when it was proposed that the instruments were tampered with. But Milton seemed much too kind and considerate to have any involvement with harm. Still, some might put his name on the list of possible perpetrators. If he were there on those particular shifts, why was his presence not noted, or was there someone, some employee, there telling Milton that he needn't watch for anything unusual? He would then make it out to be okay that that person was there. Who could that have been?

22

What has been going on with Sergeant Poley's sister, Ms. Matty Stebbins, since her trauma down in the dingy, dank, scary, slippery morgue in the basement of the Veterans Hospital? She has really done well after her fall when she almost died. Neurologically she is recovering well from the deep laceration to the skull from slipping on the concrete floor. Initially the code team was called to that department. She has not been forgotten and is receiving first-rate care. She's really a ward of the hospital for all intent and purposes mandated by the plaintiff's team for her protection. She is in a private room on the second floor and tolerating a diet with no real complaints except for some confusion as to what the next step would be. She is seen regularly by Counsel Judy Newhouse and Sandra Standstill, MD, JD, both working through Phallon and Associates.

Crystal Phallon's children are now in school, and she desired and was able to come back to work.

Matty was well enough to be discharged but really had no place to go, and no one wanted anything to adversely affect the situation of the legalities to come. Plaintiffs' depositions were taken at the Phallon and Associates offices. Defense for the VH doctors were deposed at the VH by Col. Todd Fraser, MD, JD, JAG (of the Judge Advocate General's Corps).

The $100,000 insurance policy was really of no import, a nonissue. The plaintiff, the estate of Sgt. Patrick Poley, was represented by Ms. Judy Newhouse and Sandra Standstill, MD, JD. Plaintiff was suing the Veterans Hospital and its employees, Chief Resident Rob Rogers and Intern Dr. Ronald Smith. (It was originally thought to include the medical student MS III Erin Abdulla; however, since he was not licensed and he was protected by the medical school, it would not be productive to add his name and his medical school.)

Also, being deposed by the plaintiff's team was the Teaching Hospital of New Fledgling and Dr. Friedman of the infectious diseases department. It was initially considered to add Ms. Matty Stebbins regarding her slip and fall in the morgue. As she would have nothing to add to the case, she was spared. Deep pockets in the government and the plaintiff's team was only thinking of how high the settlement should be, a golden opportunity for the two young female attorneys!

Plaintiff's case was about lack of supervision of the VH staff and delay in diagnosis and treatment of Sergeant Poley resulting in his death. The depositions were taken in New Fledgling at Phallon and Associates office. The contention was that the medical student was not supervised in the initial treatment of the patient, and he did not know how severe this disease Fournier's gangrene was. Did the student have any guidance from the intern, and did he realize there was a 50 percent mortality with this disease? He should have delayed the surgical treatment until he was properly supervised by the intern who had been called emergently away from the operating room. His treatment was totally without merit.

The intern, Dr. Smith, should have directed the student to wait until adequately supervised. Both student and intern knew nothing of the severity of this disease and should have researched the disease or had higher supervision. Alleged was that the patient should have remained in the hospital so that appropriate care was available and not discharged to be seen in seventy-two hours. That time delay led directly to the patient's death. It was alleged that Chief Resident Dr. Rogers was negligent in not supervising his intern, that he should have personally taken over the case until he could appraise himself of the patient's precarious condition. He would have seen the severity of the disease process and would have perhaps supervised the treatment appropriately. Dr. Rogers essentially was too tired to get out of bed! The patient desperately needed aggressive drainage of the abscess and debridement of dying perianal soft tissues. Again, none of the three individuals knew what they were dealing with.

Secondly, the issue of inappropriate antibacterial coverage in this lethal disease process. The patient received a dose of a cephalosporin intravenously, but this was not continued in the postoperative orders which were cosigned by Dr. Smith. That coverage was totally absent. He was on no, zero, antibiotics. At least one antibiotic should have been continued post-op, and even that would have been inadequate and inappropriate.

Then there was the issue of no specimen being submitted by the operating room staff, that cultures of the wound were done too late in the course of the disease. The phone conversation from the VH by Dr. Smith did not adequately appraise Dr. Friedman of the severity of the situation with the patient just about to die. Though Dr. Friedman waited till the next morning to see the patient was only a reflection of the staff, not realizing how desperate the situation was, and Dr. Friedman was not adequately appraised of the situation. (His name although in the record he was not adequately briefed on the patent's precarious condition, pre-code blue. His name was dropped from the case as was the Teaching Hospital of New Fledgling, and apologies would be forthcoming in writing.)

The defense in this case was essentially nil. Except that Fournier's gangrene is a rare surgical disease with a reported 50 percent mortality rate, in the best of situations no matter how aggressively it was treated. The patient, when initially stable, could have/should have been transferred to the New Fledgling medical campus right from the start. He would have been covered with several antibiotics and needed probably multiple trips to the operating room for debridement of this horrible disease and the unfortunate demise of Sergeant Poley. The defense rested its case, essentially ending the deposition. He had nothing to fire back at the attorneys! The JAG officer did not want to pursue this in court, for he had no defense. The settlement was for five million dollars.

Ms. Matty would be cared for at the government's expense with permanent lodging in living quarters at the Veterans Hospital. That was felt to be in her best interest should she agree. If she would rather return to her government-supported domicile, it would be against the hospital's concern, but she was a competent individual and might just want to be back at home with her friends with some follow-up in the days and weeks ahead. (It would be impossible to follow her two states away.) There were no winners in this case except for the plaintiff's bounty of hundreds of thousands, if not millions, of dollars of take-home pay on a nice afternoon in New Fledgling.

The big question now is, what to do with a check for five million dollars?

23

It was the next Thursday morning, and Paula, always prompt and never late for work, had been plain missing for a week. By the afternoon and no answer to their phone calls, they became genuinely concerned although they didn't want to pry into Paula's affairs. Maybe she took the weeks' vacation that she had always threatened to take. She would say it would be nice to forget about the world for a time. But she would have let them know if she were ill or for any other reason why she was not on schedule. It appeared that this was quickly becoming something that needed the help of the sheriff's department.

A female detective, Ms. Norma Paine, and a representative from the police, Sheriff Jon Langford, presented to the front desk of the Veterans Hospital and were directed to the chief of staff's office. The chief of medicine was temporarily taking over for Dr. Brice Adams as he recovered at home now from what should have been a lethal accident just over a week ago. He and Celeste were thanking God for sparing his life. Obviously, this was a miraculous recovery, and they felt that God had purpose in all of this. There must be something left to be done. Perhaps this accident and unexpected recovery would draw Brice and Celeste closer together. The passion of their marriage had cooled almost to the point of considering each other no longer as intimate but more like just getting by in the relationship. Almost becoming strangers.

As far as family, Paula had an elderly aunt, Flo Roberts. That was a dead end as she had passed away some time ago.

Sergeant Langford and the detective drove to the residence of Paula and, of course, right away noticed that her vehicle was not in the driveway. They knocked on a neighbor's door and asked if they had noticed anything unusual going on at the residence. Another dead end. They had seen her as she was leaving for work just about a week ago and wondered if she were on vacation. Another dead end!

Returning to the Veterans Hospital, each person who worked with or had any relationship with her at the Veterans Hospital was individually interviewed (interrogated) if they noticed anything unusual with Paula in the hours and days leading to the disappearance. That was a long list of people. Specifically, they wanted to know if there might have been foul play. Did she have any personal relationships outside the hospital? How was her mental status leading up to that Wednesday? Did she confide in anyone? Had she had any boyfriends or companions? Another dead end? No!

Austin confessed that they had a short-lived platonic relationship which Paula broke off rather abruptly. No argument, just sudden. And then out of fear and concern for his friend Paula, not wanting any harm to have come of her, offered some remarkably interesting information.

Austin confessed that on a Wednesday that he was off over a week ago, he came to speak with Paula to possibly get back to a friendship, apologizing as if there was something he had said or done to offend her, and of course, there was that earlier problem which she had never forgiven him for. She was in a hurry to leave which he knew would be the case. Austin was very curious, probably too curious, to know what she did on her Wednesday afternoons off. So apologetically, but wanting to help in Paula's disappearance, he confessed that he had followed her at a distance to find out what was so important with Wednesday afternoons.

After about thirty minutes, Paula turned into the parking lot of a shopping mall, and as she was getting out of her vehicle, she spotted his vehicle and him. She was furious with him because she felt that he was stalking her. She warned him to go no further or that she would call the police. Austin then left, and all he could tell the investigators was that she probably was going somewhere inside the mall. They thanked Austin, and even though he was afraid for her, the detective considered him as one of the suspects in the disappearance.

They secured and enlarged a photo of Paula. Austin let them know where the mall was located which they were aware of. Sheriff and the detective drove to that mall with the picture in hand. There were thirty-plus establishments in this mall. Where to go first? Since it was somewhat past lunchtime, they still felt that there was where they would begin. Taco Bell, a salad bar, Burger King, even at a Chinese restaurant, and no one recognized the person in the picture.

At a Chick-fil-A, one waitress recognized the picture of Paula and said that she would wait on her almost like clockwork on Wednesday afternoons and had spoken briefly with her occasionally. She said it was strange that it was two Wednesdays ago when she last saw her. This had been going on for as long as the waitress could remember, a number of years in fact. None of the other establishments in that area of the mall recognized Paula's picture. They came across a little offshoot hall where there were several businesses—Internal Revenue Service, a new dental implant office, an insurance office, and a psychologist's office. None of these businesses had seen Paula except the office staff of the psychologist. They shared offices with Dr. Donna Moss, MD, a psychiatrist. They, of course, had seen Paula often and were directed to the psychiatrist' office.

They were cautiously welcomed by a woman at the front desk. Ms. Leavitt was the doctor's office manager. There also was an LPN, Jan Crane, who asked how she could help. She was asked if she knew the person in the picture.

She responded, "What is this all about?" before saying if she knew the person in the picture.

The sheriff and the detective asked to see Dr. Donna Moss. Ms. Crane disappeared to discuss this with the psychiatrist. Several minutes went by, and finally they were ushered into the office of Dr. Moss.

They introduced themselves and asked if she knew the person in the picture. She answered that yes, and that the lady in the picture was one of her clients, but that was all the information she could divulge b/o doctor-client confidentiality. By law, that was all she had to say unless, of course, if it were a question of harm to herself or others. They told the doctor that she was a missing person now for over a week and that possibly there could be harm to her. But Dr. Moss still would only divulge a certain amount of information. They asked the doctor if she felt that Paula could be a harm to herself or others.

She replied, "You mean do I think she was suicidal or a danger to others?" No, she did not think that was the case, but that of late, her depression was becoming a bit more intense, and that lately she had been noncompliant regarding her prescribed medication. In fact, Moss had increased the dose over the past couple of weeks and that she was a no-show for her visit this Wednesday afternoon and this past Wednesday. In fact, she also missed that office visit. It was now late Thursday evening as the mall establishments were beginning to close. She now was missing for more than a week or longer.

It appeared that Dr. Moss had said all that she was required to say about her client. They were also concerned, but as it is often with these situations, they find themselves between "a rock and a hard place." That office did not do justice in this case because they had much to add, but it would only add confusion to an already bizarre case. They did not believe any information would be helpful unless she were known to be dead, but there was nothing to suggest that possibility. Still…

It was now two weeks since anyone admits to seeing Paula. Everyone at the hospital was afraid. They have just gone through these cases of patients contaminated and nearly murdered. Now the last contact of Paula was Austin in the mall parking lot two weeks ago. In fact, he was the last person to see her because she did not see the psychiatrist that very Wednesday. It appears she either changed her mind at the last minute or something had happened to her in the parking lot.

The detective wondered where Paula's vehicle was. She pulled the license plate number and traced the vehicle to a used-car lot near the police headquarters. Apparently, there was a police red sticker warning the owner to move their vehicle or it would be impounded. It had been towed away from a rental parking lot.

The attendant at the rental office was certain the picture was that of one they were interested in. They looked in a logbook to see if they had the vehicle there and, if so, when it was brought in. In fact, they did have the vehicle in the police salvage lot. It was brought in directly from an accident scene a couple of weeks ago. It was a rental and had been rented to a Sondra Barnes. The vehicle was totaled in the accident. They had no information about the victims in the accident. That was none of their business, but the Teaching Hospital in New Fledgling might have some information as it was near an off-ramp heading for New Fledgling.

Apparently, Paula had parked her vehicle in the rental lot. Just as a Sondra Barnes had also rented a vehicle. Paula's vehicle had been towed away to a used-car lot since it had been unclaimed. There would be a police notation somewhere as there would have been a warning posted on the vehicle by the police department for the owner to move their vehicle. Often unclaimed vehicles belong to suspicious individuals. For instance, you would not expect a vehicle with a pro-life license plate to be in the middle of a heavy drug trafficking neighborhood! So every vehicle and license plate have a history, like a set of fingerprints.

24

It has been over two weeks since Brice's accident and emergency surgery. He has been recovering at home, a miraculous recovery without a doubt in his wife's heart and mind. The effectual fervent prayer of the righteous availeth much. Dr. Celeste Adams, Brice's wife, a pediatric surgeon at the Teaching Hospital in New Fledgling, was back to her heavy schedule as Brice didn't need her help at this point at home. He was totally in the dark regarding his wife's growing relationship with Laura, the director of nursing. He had thought he had seen the two together as he was recovering from the anesthesia of the first emergency surgery. (You will recall that the special instrument tray wrapped with red cloth was used in Brice's surgical procedure.)

Brice was feeling stronger every day and decided to take a ride. He drove to the golf course where everyone knew Dr. Brice and Sondra would be every Wednesday afternoon for quite some time. Brice explained where he had been, about the accident and surgery, and how well he was doing. They asked how Sondra was, for they had not seen her for a couple of Wednesdays. He did not know, and he had no way of getting in touch with her—no phone number, no address. She had always just met him there. It was their secret.

The sheriff and the detective made a visit to New Fledgling and the Teaching Hospital, and at the front desk, they asked the volunteer to look if Paula had been a patient. Paula's name was not in their computer. So she had not been involved in any accident and had not been a patient at the hospital. They already had checked the police records and run into a dead end. Paula had just disappeared. Three weeks into the disappearance of Paula. This was quickly becoming a "cold case."

They decided to go back to the beginning and searched Paula's home. First, asking neighbors if they had seen her back at her home. They had not spent much time there because they had no notion that this was a crime scene. It just appeared unremarkable as from the beginning. Looking through the drawers of the dresser, the detective looked in the top drawer and found something that might be helpful. Inside a wool stocking was a beeper! But what would they do with it? There was no information on the beeper. How do they trace a beeper? Was the battery still functioning? They removed the dead double-A battery and replaced it with a fresh battery. There was a message on the beeper, an apparent phone number.

Detective Norma Paine was becoming obsessed with Paula. Sheriff Langford checked with the department who the number belonged to. However, there was no area code associated with the number, so they just used the local area code and found that the number belonged to Dr. Felix Fitzgerald, a hypnotherapist in New Fledgling, at the location of Dr. Moss. They arranged a trip together back to the mall. It was 1:00 p.m., Wednesday afternoon. It was not the same person at the reception desk. They asked if Dr. Moss were in, and they were told that she left a couple of hours ago and asked if Dr. Fitzgerald could help them. They were ushered into the same plush office when they had seen Dr. Moss. Only thing different was the office staff. They waited about twenty minutes, and then the doctor came in, and he asked them if he could be of assistance. He apologized for the delay, but he was in a session with a client.

At the police department, as they were checking the phone number 933 3645 and finding it a cell phone number associated with a doctor, they traced the good *doctor's* record with state licensing bureaus. They found that the doctor had his license revoked in two other states and had been charged with being an accessory to an unsolved murder case. That was yet to be revealed to the sheriff and the detective.

The doctor stated that he had an active clientele in another city in the state and that he was only there for just the one afternoon a week. He offered what he primarily was involved with, that being tobacco, alcohol, and drug addiction, but primarily he used hypnosis for many weight-loss patients, successfully he added. They asked to see the names of the patients he saw at that location. He was hesitant to offer that information, but after they told him they were involved in a cold case, possible homicide, he asked his nurse to get the logbook of Wednesday afternoon's patients. There were only four names in the book. Three men and one woman named Sondra Barnes who was being treated with hypnosis for PTSD. They pulled out the folded photo of Paula Hunter, and he said the person in the picture looked very much like that of Sondra Barnes. It was a picture of Paula Hunter. They were getting so close! He offered no further information, and furthermore, he asked them to leave. But they didn't leave empty handed. They had the name of someone who looked like Paula Hunter. It was getting crazy to dance around this doctor. They were unaware of his losing his license in two states. The doctor offered one more bit of information. Sondra Barnes had missed her last three office visits. That she had not canceled, just was a no-show. They had no personal information, and there was no answer to a number they called. Who was Sondra Barnes?

Back to a fresh start with a new name. At the salvage yard near the police department, the wrecked rental vehicle was traced to Sondra Barnes. At the rental company, Sondra Barnes's name came up as to having a rental contract signed by a Sondra Barnes about three weeks ago. It had just been signed out for twenty-four hours and had not been returned.

Checking back with the department, they gave him information regarding a Felix Fitzgerald who had lost his license and was involved as an accessory to an unsolved murder case in another state. For a price, it appears that Fitzgerald can use his hypnotherapy for remarkably interesting purposes depending upon the wishes of his client. Sure, he had the weight-loss gig going for him, but that was peanuts compared to the moneys, never claimed by the IRS. We are talking about ten to twenty thousand dollars and the use of hypnosis when foul play was suspected or anticipated.

As part of his extraordinarily strong hypnotic powers, he provided a beeper where he could contact the patient...part of the hypnosis gig and signaling the client to proceed with the overpowering suggestion. His specialty involved missing persons. (Was he not wanted in other states by a different name? A mad scientist.)

Patients, when hypnotized, would assume another identity, carry out the deed, and then afterward would disappear. Was this the case here? Perhaps Paula was hypnotized becoming Sondra, and with some cosmetic changes, she became a different person. Sondra rented a vehicle, and she played golf with Brice every Wednesday. She wanted Brice all to herself, and on a fateful Wednesday afternoon, she had headed for the Teaching Hospital in New Fledgling to confess to Brice's wife, Dr. Celeste Adams, a pediatric surgeon, that she was having an affair with her husband, even though platonic, a developing friendship.

Sondra rented a vehicle and was emotionally distraught about what she planned to do. She seemed to be in some identity crisis as in *The Outer Limits.* She was beside herself, crying so hard that she couldn't see through the tears well as she was about to enter the interstate. Brice had followed her to stop her from seeing his wife and gave a little bump to her back bumper, trying just to get her attention. Hard to do at seventy miles per hour. The bump caused the rollover of the rental, and the rest was history.

The only real information of grave importance was what happened to Sondra. Another trip to the hospital asking at the front desk if Sondra Barnes was in the computer. In fact, she was for just one day. She was brought to the hospital after the accident but transferred from Trauma Institute across the hall to the Transplant Institute where she was found to be brain-dead, and she was donor of heart and kidneys. The only outstanding information was that no one had claimed the body which remained in a frozen drawer in the morgue until further information was available.

Do we have one missing individual in Paula, two missing individuals in Paula and Sondra or was Paula/Sondra one missing person with two identities? Both individuals were missing at the exact same time. The detective considered how to solve the dilemma. They asked for volunteers who knew Paula very well to accompany them to the morgue at the Teaching Hospital back in New Fledgling. The chief of staff knew Paula very well, and he was volunteered to help solve the mystery. He was an extremely reluctant *volunteer* but agreed to help identify the remains. Two other individuals from the OR at the VH agreed to help. They all met that afternoon around drawer 3 in the morgue. It was a chilling situation, but of all things, everyone agreed that the remains could be that of Paula Young or possibly a look-alike. Brice offered no opinion. What was certain was that Brice found himself very confused. Sondra and Paula could pass for twins.

25

It happened nearly a month ago that Paula's remains were identified. Milton Conover had been asked to come in late on a Sunday night. His brother, Professor Delbert Conover, was not thrilled about this situation with Milton acting in any capacity as a security guard. He was untrained and would only be a body looking for anything unusual on the second floor of the Veterans Hospital. About 9:45 p.m., the floor was quiet as a church mouse, but he was startled to hear the swinging doors of the surgical suite being opened. To his knowledge, there was no reason for anybody to enter the surgery department this time of night. He didn't quite know what to make of it, so he found the whereabouts of the night nursing supervisor and explained what he had heard. There were no emergency cases that she was aware of. Probably someone retrieving something which they had left behind.

It was dark in the suite except for the red running lights along the baseboards. There was, however, a light in Central Supply. Not wishing to disturb anyone with business there, they kept quiet as they approached Central Supply. There was an individual with their back to them, wearing a long white lab jacket. They held their breath, not to be discovered, wishing to see what the individual was doing. They were apparently spraying some solution onto a tray of instruments. They were not noticed yet. But startled, the individual turned to face them…Paula or Laura?

Wait just a minute. The remains of Paula Hunter were identified by close coworkers and reluctantly by Brice Adams in the morgue at the Teaching Hospital one month ago. Paula disappeared one month ago. Laura could never stand a trial without proof that all cases were *doctored* by the same individual. And for that matter, Brice had hesitated in identifying the deceased because he thought that it was the person he called Sondra. Sondra, golfing partner, diner date every Wednesday afternoon and evening for the past two years. And what was the motive in the first place? Whoever did it? Insane jealousy?

What kind of relationship did the identical twins have with one another? It appears that they were closer than anyone knew. They even had the same days off work, Wednesday afternoon and evening. And more importantly, they shared the same therapist for the post-traumatic stress disorder stemming from the fatal crash at ten years of age. Paula knew Sondra well and was desperately frightened by her *alter* for that is what Sondra was, a conniving victim of dissociative identity disorder (DID) or more commonly known as multiple personality disorder, but Sondra was the stronger personality. Paula loved Brice Adams, but Sondra loved him more and was willing to tell of the affair though it truly was platonic.

Brice and Sondra had a heated argument on the golf course. Sondra, fuming mad, wanted more than just eighteen holes of golf and diner. That was why and where Sondra was speedily heading to the Teaching Hospital to tell all to Celeste Adams. Brice followed her rented vehicle and was trying desperately to stop Sondra but not on a four-lane highway. Sondra thought that if she could get rid of Paula, she could have Brice alone. She didn't take into consideration that with Paula out of the way, Sondra would die as well. Brice miraculously survived. Sondra and Paula are both missing.

With the two of them dead, the director of nursing, a close friend of Celeste's, unmarried, unattached Laura was free to show her true feelings toward Celeste, a secret no one knew. At first, Laura's desire for Celeste in the beginning was for her friendship. They would see each other nearly every day. Celeste was becoming more and more distant from her husband. They spent little time together, and when they were together, they were exhausted and slept in separate rooms. Ships in the night! Celeste needed the friendship and company of someone and that was someone who could fill the void of a marriage literally vanishing.

At first, Laura's desire for Celeste was unrequited, but they were together every day. Their offices were next to one another. They shared important committees together. They found themselves being drawn together as a magnet. Their touching, perhaps only shoulder to shoulder, began to wear on the heartstrings of the two of them. Then they found themselves together more and more as the days went by.

Laura and Celeste's relationship blossomed when the two of them were at the bedside of Brice as he struggled to survive a near-fatal accident. Celeste needed a shoulder to cry on during that emotional time at his bedside. Laura was there, and then there were their thoughts toward one another. It would eventually lead to unscheduled time together, they had *D* the desire, unnatural toward one another, culminating in a love relationship. They had become obsessed with one another, and no one knew. They wanted to be together more and more.

26

Norma Paine and Sheriff Jon Langford obtained a search warrant and drove to the mall they had visited prior where Austin had directed them. They passed the Internal Revenue Service Office, the dental implant office, the Prudential Insurance Office, and moved on to Dr. Moss and Dr. Fitzgerald's office. Dr. Moss's office was empty with a sign on the window, "For Rent." The office was cleaned out, empty with no forwarding address!

It appeared our professional health care workers had very suddenly slipped away. No idea where they had gone or why they had gone so quickly. The hypnotherapist was on the lamb, running away or fleeing, as from the law—fugitives, vagabonds, elusive. Apparently, the information they had been privy to was old news. It had happened in at least two other locales or states. The next step was some deep detective work. Which states were they also running from? Medical boards across the nation were being queried particularly those who's jurisdictions were nearby. The name Felix Fitzgerald was so unusual that it should be easy to trace, if that was truly the "doctor's" real name.

During their visit at this location, they never saw any diplomas or licenses on the wall, and they hadn't asked for any proof that he was a legitimate physician or never really crossed their mind that he was just a physician but a *hypnotherapist*. That should had been food for thought, but they missed the opportunity.

It should be easy using the internet and the name Felix Fitzgerald. Wrong, no such provider by that name. He must have just used that alias for the first time. So now we just ask each state medical board for any physician suspicious of being an accessory to murder or involved in a missing person while being a so-called *hypnotherapist*. Or perhaps Donna Moss was the real person on the lamb.

Querying the boards of medicine was productive. There were three by that name, only one a psychologist. Research discovered her starting a new practice in another state and came to find out she advertised herself as a nutritionist and a hypnotherapist. Getting warm or piping hot?

Next step was to ask if there was a medical doctor in her office whose specialty was hypnotherapy. Dr. Moss worked fast. It just so happens that Dr. Vane Patrick shared the office with Dr. Moss two days a week, Tuesday and Thursday. The board in that state had no record of any Vane Patrick, apparently another alias. Dr. Moss's secretary was asked when they could see Dr. Vane Patrick. She suggested that they call his cell (no pun intended) phone to make an appointment as he had yet to be seen in their office. The number they were given was 933-3645! They dialed the number, and the recorder told them that number was no longer in service.

26.2

Epilogue DOA

No, not "dead on arrival." There is an old black-and-white movie by that title, staring Edmund O'Brien in 1950. Someone had poisoned O'Brien. But there are three ingredients, three components to any crime: *desire*, *opportunity*, and *ability*. I'll try to explain it. It is a bit complicated so follow closely as I will be backtracking some. Maybe even I might figure it out.

Paula and Laura were closer than anyone will ever know. You see, everything revolved around Laura. How is that you ask because we haven't heard one thing about her since she was ten years old? You see, Laura was director of nursing services at the Teaching Hospital in New Fledgling. She worked extremely hard to obtain that position and was proud of that. Her desire, however, was for Dr. Celeste Adams the Pediatric Surgeon at the same Teaching Hospital and wife of Dr. Brice Adams at the VH. This desire was fed daily by the proximity of the two women. Both Celeste and Laura had never confessed that love to one another. It was a slow process.

Loneliness, accessibility led to desire for someone to fill the void in their lives. Each were starving to be wanted, to be desired with no outlet. Both were attractive women in the late forties. The relationship was destined to grow as they saw each other daily. In desperate moments, Laura found herself daydreaming about herself and Celeste. What stood in her way if Celeste had feelings for her? Her obsession included the roadblock of Brice, to have him out of the picture and to discredit him anyway she could. He was nearing reassignment and would take Celeste with him. That could never be!

Paula wanted to lose a little weight, and through her friends, they suggested a weight control *doctor* in New Fledgling who used hypnotic therapy. Paula had, for a long time, been under the care of psychiatrists for her PTSD and was on medication, which had helped her tremendously. Paula was leery of the idea and quite frankly afraid of hypnosis. She knew nothing about this therapist. She had asked Laura to go with her to the first half dozen sessions to sort of hold her hand. Laura needed to see the truth of clinical hypnosis.

If you will recall, Laura has a bachelor's degree in psychology and a master's degree in clinical/abnormal psychology which, of course, would have included a time practicing the clinical procedure of hypnosis as part of her training, but that was twenty years ago. She needed a refresher course, and the timing was perfect for her. This hypnotherapist had a technique associated with suggestion therapy which could manipulate people, and that was with the use of cell phone and the archaic beeper. Whenever the *therapist* used suggestion therapy, it was keyed to a link (therapist's phone) and the patient (or victim). For instance, at the lunch hour, the beeper could go off *suggesting* that the patient recall she is not to eat certain foods, likewise at suppertime. Admittedly, it could be costly, but a habit would be formed, and the phone/beeper would no longer be needed.

Unfortunately, Paula had another mental problem of DID (dissociative identity disorder) which was stimulated by the hypnosis. Paula's *alter* was Sondra, a stronger personality, not at all pleased with what was being suggested to Paula. She was happy the way things were and was very reluctant to any change, and she recognized the phone/beeper, and it brought her out as well. For instance, every Wednesday at 2:30 p.m. after Paula's visit, Paula became Sondra with a change to tight clothing, wig, and excessive makeup. She was a different person. This happened Wednesdays, and somehow, she ended up playing golf with Brice, having dinner with him, and that was the extent, perfectly platonic. This also happened on Sunday evenings, Paula becoming Sondra. The power of suggestion courtesy of a timely beep!

What has this to do with dear Laura who desired what was the unrequited love of Celeste Adams? Laura wanted Brice out of the picture entirely—*desire*, our first ingredient in DOA. She was quite often with Celeste and enamored of her. She had no limit as to what she would do to discredit Brice Adams, COS. Laura was in love with Celeste.

In comes the second ingredient in crime, *opportunity*. Remember Laura is an identical twin of sister Paula's. She could pass for Paula and, as a result, could come and go at the Veterans Hospital without question and without anyone's suspicion. Paula also loved Brice Adams but not as deeply as Sondra, a deeper, stronger personality. This Wednesday occurrence of golf and diner had been going on for quite some time. After Paula's visit to the hypnotherapist, she became Sondra for only Wednesday afternoons. His wife, Celeste, and Brice had terribly busy schedules, and so busy, they were the proverbial ships passing in the night.

Oblivious to Wednesday's activities, Celeste had no idea. If Paula possessed the beeper, for dietary purposes, at precise times, it brought out Sondra. At 2:30 p.m., each Wednesday, Sondra was with Brice and wanted more than just golf and dinner, which was out of the question and out of timing. Brice and Sondra had a heated argument during the golf game. Sondra stormed away stating she was going to inform Celeste of Wednesday's goings-on. She drove to a car rental office, parked the car (Paula's), rented a car just for a day, and headed to the Teaching Hospital to inform Celeste of their *affair*. You will find that Laura also has the necessary *A* for *ability* in the end.

Brice followed closely behind her to the interstate, trying to get her attention, to stop her. Unfortunately, you now know what happened. Paula/Sondra, emotional in tears, was *touched* on the right rear bumper. At the accident, Paula/Sondra were thrown out the windshield as the car rolled, and Brice was near fatally injured as well. Paula/Sondra became organ donors by law because of brain death. Brice survived. He was supposed to die along with Sondra. Laura had been responsible for the contaminated instruments. *Ability*, the third ingredient to any crime. She knew exactly what she was doing. The third time was when Mr. Conover was doing a special job one late Sunday night, and Laura was caught.

She claimed that Paula had been responsible for the first two incidents, and what Laura did was short of any crime because the instruments were never used. Nonetheless, Laura was arrested and charged with ten counts of attempted manslaughter. She, of course, pleaded not guilty. Circumstantial evidence was introduced, and regardless, Laura was given consecutive life sentences. She was jailed pending appeal.

To further prove of this, the detective Norma Paine and Sheriff Jon Langford searched Laura's home. In the basement, there was a small laboratory. Beneath the hood of the laboratory were several Petri dishes with extensive growth of what proved to be bacteria from Sergeant Poley's perirectal abscess, essentially proving Laura's guilt.

Epilogue

Their lives were spent on careers so exhaustive, pulling them apart 24-7. Similar marriages would quite often burn away the love that they so preciously vowed now turned cold. Not so with the Michaels family. Their love for Christ kept them together with Jesus as the centerpiece. At one point, they yearned for rest, for a place together to experience quiet sunrise and sunsets. Giving them pause to look forward to retirement should that ever really happen, so…they bought an island.

Sunrise, sunset
Sunrise, sunset
Swiftly flow the days
Seedlings turn overnight to sunflowers.

Blossoming even as we gaze
Sunrise, sunset
Sunrise, sunset
Swiftly fly the years
One season following another
Laden with happiness and tears

So they purchased Drayton Island, a privately owned heavily wooded island at the northern end of Lake George on the west side of the Saint John's River's main channel in Putnam County, Florida, located at the northern edge of Lake George about twenty miles south of Palatka, their piece of earth modest in size is surrounded by the Saint John's River. With a history dating back to the Native Americans of Central Florida, Drayton has seen its share of explorers, slaves, plantation owners, and ordinary residents who have moved there to grow crops, fish, and enjoy a truly idyllic life. He was the son of William Drayton Sr., who served as justice of the province of East Florida (1765–1780). The island was developed as a plantation when William Drayton Sr., a migrant from South Carolina, bought it along with other properties in Florida. He was nominated by President George Washington on June 11, 1790, to a seat on the United States District Court for the District of South.

George and Lisa built a home on their island to experience God's nature all about them. So secluded you can't see it on the map, not even on GPS.

It was also a place to gather festively. And the first business was to thank him for the life of Valerie at one point so close to death. God truly allowed them to celebrate her surviving a near catastrophic surgical illness. So they celebrated her life on Drayton Island.

Thereafter, they also celebrated the life of Rexford Swiss, closing a thirty-two-year saga of the town of Fledgling. An interesting passage from death to life. Dr. Swiss, the first real general surgeon, hung on and participated in the new birth of a rural American town. It had its first infant cries. Dr. Suzanne Grayson was there forever grateful to God for the salvation of 2008 where the story begins.

Hannah and Alex's unfolding lives in the end miraculously with a story out of Scripture with Joseph and his brothers… God meant it for good. We have watched as modern medicine and surgery brought new life to Fledgling. God was honored as we saw Dr. Mullen escape colon cancer and never a recurrence of the disease. We have seen drug addiction snuff out the life of Dr. Snowden but restoring the health of many because of his death.

We have seen this area of land grow with the time. Lives challenged and changed, lost being saved, God's name honored. Out of the dust, we watched twenty-first-century medicine and surgery come alive. There is everlasting hope, and as a small town, it finally has its airport to land by the lighted cross of a hospital. And Alex's new biology textbook, his son given new life from Alex's spare kidney.

Together
With their families

Valerie
Anne Michaels
and
Keith
Franklin Meadows

Invite you to their
Wedding ceremony
December 26, 2044
Four o'clock in the afternoon

Drayton Island
Crescent City, Florida

Dinner and Dancing to Follow

About the Authors

Jack Weitzel, MD, FACS, MABS, MCEd, is a retired general surgeon and a founding trustee of Evangelical College and Seminary. He is married to Melinda, his high school sweetheart. They have four grown children and seven grandchildren. They live in Zephyrhills, Florida. He has authored six books.

Michael Weitzel, RT at Edwards Lifesciences. Lisa Weitzel, RN, CRM, at Abbott, St. Jude. Michael and Lisa live in Jacksonville, Florida. They have three grown children.

Dr. Ken Weitzel is retired chiropractor, who had a thirty-year practice in Orlando. Ken has two grown daughters and lives in Plant City, Florida. Ken and Jack are both Vietnam veterans.

CPSIA information can be obtained
at www.ICGtesting.com
Printed in the USA
LVHW020730290322
714676LV00001B/134

9 781685 174361